The Lost Library of the Tsar

JT OSBOURNE

1

Brook Burlington stood on the stage before a row of bright lights and tried to remember what she was doing there. Despite having given dozens of talks in the past year, a crippling feeling of nervousness surged through her body. She felt her throat tighten. Butterflies fluttered in her stomach, her breath coming in shallow gasps.

The glare from the stage surprised her, as did the smallness of both the stage itself and the audience—a few hundred people. She'd seen a couple of these Ideas Forum talks online, generally when one of her colleagues insisted she look at something they felt was groundbreaking. It was a great honor, Brook had been told, to be asked to speak, and she had been sincerely flattered, but now she felt small and petty, stranded on a tiny stage with some sort of microphone headset attached to her head. In the reflection of the TV cameras, she thought she looked stupid and helpless—like a deer in the headlights with a junior-high student's embarrassing orthodontic contraption all over her face.

She took a sip of water to steady her nerves and breathing. The stage manager counted down with his fingers as the announcer gave her introduction, "Brook Burlington, Distinguished Professor at West Virginia University, holder of the prestigious Amelia B. Edwards Chair, discoverer of the Lost Tomb of Cleopatra, daughter of renowned archaeologist Cale Burlington—"

Blah blah blah—Brook was sick of it by now. They were feeding off her, all of them, and she felt every bite. She was famous now, and just beginning to understand what that meant; life in the spotlight, endless travel, speaking engagements, an additional workload both in the wider university and within the department, and visitors from all over the world stopping by her office at Woodburn Hall just to be associated with her. Hundreds of emails came in each day from students and faculty worldwide, media outlets, and historical organizations. One of Brook's PhD students was tied up nearly full-time politely responding to requests of one sort or another. She was more in demand than ever, all because she'd been lucky and found a bunch of royal bones in a two-thousand-year-old crypt somewhere near the Egypt-Libya border, where nobody had bothered to look before...

Finding Cleopatra had been her life's work, and by anybody's yardstick, a tremendous achievement, but lately Brook found herself minimizing the accomplishment far beyond mere modesty, mocking it even, to protect herself from her growing fear—what if that's all you ever do?

"Good evening," Brook began, finding her voice and looking

out over the crowd, quickly falling into rote recitation. She'd given this speech every semester to every undergraduate class she'd taught in the last decade—there had been no time to prepare, and she was too exhausted to come up with anything new and fresh. She'd dubbed it her "Why Archaeology Matters" speech, which was a lot like the more recent "Why Colleges and Universities Matter" speech she'd given at three different high school graduation ceremonies over the past Spring.

Brook's argument was that Mankind was ultimately responsible for three things, the continuation of life on Earth, the protection of all knowledge—past and present—and the expansion of knowledge.

"Of course, you don't need to go to college to procreate," she would tell the high school students with a wink, which would always get a laugh, "but you might want to know something about biology, the environment, chemistry, business, politics, and medicine if you want your children to have half a chance."

Brook skipped that section this time. "The continuation of life on Earth" didn't seem so important to her now. In fact, she was leaning towards a "maybe humans don't deserve to live" philosophy; based on her own reading of the world from the depressed state she'd recently found herself stuck in.

"Colleges and Universities are not designed to teach young people 'careers,' or help them find 'jobs,'" Brook proclaimed. "Sure, there are Nursing Schools and Engineering Schools and Agriculture Schools, but learning particular skills for a career is only a side-line to the main business of higher education, which is passing on the wisdom of our species to a new generation while exploring, researching, revising, and expanding that wisdom. Archaeology is the attempt to accumulate and organize the wisdom of all humanity through the ages—uncovering all the wisdom we can find."

Brook supposed she finished the speech well—there was applause at the end, she noted—but she'd been distracted by seeing a tall, thin man in the audience. He stood past the lights, towards the back, seemingly trying to stay hidden so as not to distract her.

Of course you'd show up here.

Brook was sure it was Tom Manor. Even though she hadn't seen him in over a year, she had been spotting him in all sorts of places recently, in mistaken public sightings as well as in her dreams.

"Excellent! Nicely said," the producer of the show assured Brook as she stepped off the stage. The stage lights went out, and the audience began filing out of the back. Brook could feel members of that audience surging toward her, clamoring for an autograph, to ask a question, or just connect somehow.

Brook ran.

The dressing room was a closet, really, but it was supposed to be her sanctuary, or so Brook hoped. When she stepped inside, she gasped and held back a scream. On the dressing table was a canopic jar—about ten inches tall and perfect—no doubt authentic. From her first glance, she was certain it had been taken from the lost tomb of Cleopatra.

2

"It's beautiful, isn't it?" Tom Manor remarked.

"I'll give you that," Brook told him. She sat on a small sofa in the dressing room, stunned and trying to catch her breath.

"You got the falcon," Tom remarked. The ceramic jar's carved wood head depicted the god Qebehsenuef, one of the four sons of Horus. "Which means..." Tom said, allowing Brook to answer.

"...I got the intestines."

"Lucky you," Tom quipped. "I got the baboon."

Brook stared at him, not sure what exactly was going on—a feeling she'd been experiencing more and more since falling into Cleopatra's tomb.

"Did you send this to me?" Brook asked.

Tom shook his head.

"Not me. But I got one just like it—part of the same set, I believe."

They both knew what that meant. There would be four canopic

jars in all, identical to those buried with every Egyptian nobleman up to a certain period. Each depicted a different god and contained a different organ. Hapi, the baboon, held the lungs; Duamutef, the jackal, carried the stomach; Imsety, the human, contained the liver, and Qebehsenuef, the falcon, which Brook had received, held the intestines.

"You got one from who… whom?" Brook shook her head, still confused.

"No idea," Tom said lightly, as if this was some type of parlor game, "but it popped up just like yours did."

Brook just nodded. She was too exhausted to deal with this.

"Let me drive you home," Tom suggested.

"Home?" Brook answered, unsure of where that was, or even where *she* was at the moment.

"Back to your hotel. You're flying out tomorrow, right?"

"That's right," Brook answered, getting her bearings. She was in San Francisco—well, near San Francisco, in Silicon Valley. "I'm staying near the airport."

"I have a rental car."

"They gave me a driver," Brook managed to get out. "He's probably waiting in that big black car right outside."

"Sweet," Tom said.

"Yeah," Brook responded with a faint smile. "Sweet."

"I'll help you out," Tom said, offering his arm.

Brook stood, established she wasn't going to pass out, and then took Tom's arm.

"Can you get the jar?" she asked.

"I got it," Tom answered, picking it up and nestling it under his arm like a fullback.

"If I fall—" Brook said.

"I got you," Tom reassured her.

"—save the *jar*," Brook finished with conviction.

Tom laughed.

"Okay. Will do. Jar first, tired lady second."

They walked to the curb. Even this long after the lecture, people lingered to thank Professor Burlington for her speech, for coming, and for finding Cleopatra's remains. Despite her obvious debilitation, Brook managed to be gracious to each and every one before collapsing in the back of the limousine. Tom handed her the canopic jar and she carefully buckled it in on the seat next to her.

"It was nice to see you again, Tom," Brook said softly, touching the younger man's hand, half holding, half shaking it. She truly meant it, and Tom was moved by the gesture. He could only imagine what she'd been through since they'd last been together in the Libyan Desert. Brook, meanwhile, saw the hopelessness on Tom's face—he so obviously wanted to help her, and to be with her, but she was nowhere near ready. "See you later." She released his hand, grabbed the door-handle, and closed the door on him. Before Tom could say anything, the car drifted out into the night.

*   *   *

"May I help you?"

"Yes, I need to buy an extra seat," Brook told the customer service representative at the San Francisco International Airport the next morning. At first, she put the jar up on the counter, then decided to hold it instead.

Earthquake country, she reminded herself.

"Name of the passenger?" the ticket woman asked, clacking on her keyboard, eyes fixed on her computer screen.

"Uh, no name," Brook responded.

"Federal regulations require—"

"It's for this," Brook stated, holding up the jar for the woman to see. Brook suddenly wondered if security would force her to open it—she'd avoided that so far—and if they did, what they would make of three-thousand-year-old intestines. Depending on the age of the jar—Brook still wasn't *exactly* sure how old it was—and the skill of the embalmer, the intestines could very well be nearly intact.

"I can move you up one row so you and your...item...can sit together."

"Great," Brook replied.

"That'll be two hundred and fifty-seven—" the agent started to say. "Wait, are those human remains?" she asked confidentially, lowering her voice.

"Actually, yes," Brook admitted. "Is that allowed?"

"Certainly," the woman answered. "Just not in checked luggage. Most just put them in the overhead bin, though."

Brook felt like making a quip about her "Aunt Sally" being claustrophobic, but decided this was no place to be joking. Telling anyone that this was a priceless ancient relic wouldn't be prudent either.

"The full price is two fifty-seven, but I can give you our

bereavement fare?" the agent said.

Brook stifled a laugh and nodded.

"One hundred and ninety-five, then," the ticket agent said.

"I'll take it," Brook answered, painfully holding back laughter as she handed her credit card over.

The ticket agent glanced up as she took the card, unsure of Brook's sanity.

"I am so sorry for your loss. Have a good flight," the woman offered sincerely, handing over her extra ticket.

Once on board, Brook looked forward to three hours of airborne quiet and solitude with a window to lean her head against. The businessman in the aisle seat only seemed interested in his laptop; he hadn't remarked on or even appeared to notice the ancient Egyptian jar between him and Brook, which also meant he wasn't aware that Brook was the world-famous discoverer of the lost tomb of Cleopatra and Antony.

Brook checked her watch. She'd be home in time to make it to her office—the new one with a window and view of the Monongahela River, the university's way of saying thanks. Brook had caught herself staring out of that window between classes more and more lately.

Exhaustion, she told herself. *All you need is sleep.*

A couple of times she'd found herself on the floor; passed out, she guessed.

Lately she had been thinking about seeing someone about everything that was happening to her.

A doctor? Maybe I'll get a referral to someone...a psychiatrist, or psychologist.

She suppressed the thought, both dreading and hoping her present state might be physical.

Vitamin deficiency, hormonal imbalance—something with a "take one of these every morning" fix.

Disease could be cured, but mental illness? She didn't know.

Brook shivered as the plane took off, soaring east to an uncertain future.

If there was just somebody to talk to...

A natural introvert, Brook had always embraced solitude, but as she had become busier and busier over the last year, she'd also found herself becoming more and more lonely. There wasn't time in her life for herself, let alone for anyone else. Her classes were filled to the brim, and the PhD candidates she'd hired as TAs hadn't been much help, or in some cases even worth the trouble.

TA stands for Time Abyss, she had decided.

She was still obsessed with Cleopatra, keeping track of the squabbles about where her remains and the artifacts would end up. Technically, they'd been discovered in Libya, but nobody could deny that the burial artifacts of the last Pharaoh were part of Egyptian history and culture. She had weighed in and she had worried, but ultimately she had no power, and her opinion was just that, an opinion.

"Everyone's got one," she'd been told on more than one occasion.

She patted the jar next to her. That was yet another disturbing mystery.

What would Dad say?

Brook's father, Cale Burlington, a *legend* in the field of treasure diving, had never been troubled by self-doubt, at least not until the last. Hardened by the Marine Corps, Cale had mined the seven seas for gold and artifacts without much of a care, or so it had always seemed to her.

Now, though, she wondered if that was true. Who knew what went on in a man's mind, especially when he was your father, and played the part of the swashbuckling plunderer?

He was a good actor, Brook admitted. *Maybe he even fooled himself.*

At the end, after it had all collapsed, Brook had seen a different side of the man she worshipped and had tried all her life to emulate. He had terrified her then. His friends had betrayed him; he'd been snookered, outsmarted, beaten. Everything decent about the man had been used against him, all humanity torn from his heart.

"The lungs, the liver, the stomach, and the intestines are all needed in the afterlife," Brook muttered to herself as the jet reached cruising altitude. "There is no jar for the heart, however. The heart is the seat of the soul, so it is left inside the body."

The businessman in the aisle seat kept his eyes on his laptop and pretended he hadn't heard a thing.

That was okay with Brook.

3

Somewhere near Halat Ammar, British Transjordan, 1918

The pickets stayed on high alert through the dark night. In addition to the regular guard, 90 personal bodyguards protected the life of Colonel T.E. Lawrence, whose exploits against the Ottoman Turks had generated a hefty bounty on his head. The guards were nervous on this particular moonless night, and an unsteady breeze blew in from the Sinai. The loyalty of Lawrence's troops was unquestionable, but as the rumored reward for his death soared, the possibility of a greedy traitor in the ranks also grew.

There had been many assassination attempts made against Lawrence already, all from the outside, and all miserable failures, mostly because the Ottomans had no idea what he actually looked like, so successful was the British Army's effort to keep his appearance secret. As Lawrence defeated the Ottomans in battle after battle, the legend grew, and so did the reward.

Nobody stepping into camp would ever expect that the scruffy 5-foot, 5-inch Brit walking briskly around camp was actually the famed fighter.

"Intruder at two o'clock!" came the shout from one of the guards.

Rifles were readied. The shape of some four-legged beast— either a camel or horse, it was too far to tell at this distance—was just visible on the horizon, followed by a second shape behind it.

Binoculars were brought to bear.

"Looks like one of ours!" came the announcement from the British Second Lieutenant in charge.

No rifle sagged, no finger poised on a trigger relaxed. Both the British and their Arab allies under the command of Auda Abu Tayi understood this could be a trick of some sort.

"Man on horseback, and he's got a bloody prisoner," the man with the binoculars muttered to the Second Lieutenant and the others closest around him.

"Blow the whistle!" his commander bellowed crisply.

The signalman gave two short toots followed by one long blast on his whistle, piercing the silence of the night. Three short whistles came back; the correct return signal on this particular watch.

"Bloody clever, this assassin," the British officer remarked. Not a single man along the perimeter moved; no-one believed this was anything other than a diabolical ruse.

"It's Hastings!" someone called out as the figure drew closer.

"Easy, men!" the Second Lieutenant ordered, privately relieved. Lance Corporal Reggie Hastings was a trusted scout, generally out on night patrol far beyond the perimeter. The man was loyal and brave, frequently going above the call of duty, but he wasn't crazy. Even at gunpoint, he wouldn't bring a traitor into camp.

"Found him approaching on foot," Corporal Hastings told the night-watch commander after he was let into camp. He nodded to the one-armed prisoner whose lone hand was tied with rope, the other end of which Hastings held in his hand. "He was carrying this." Hastings gingerly handed over an oak box measuring around five feet long and ornately decorated. "Says it's a gift for Commander Lawrence."

"Sappers!" the Second Lieutenant called.

A trio of engineers stepped up, and after some discussion, it was decided that the Bedouin himself would open the box at gunpoint, clear of camp by a hundred yards.

"If it's a bomb, he blows himself up," they decided.

"And if it's not, we can still shoot him," one of the sappers reasoned.

Sharpshooters—both Arab and British—aimed from a distance at the man who called himself Isa bin Khalid bin Isa Huwaytati as he opened the box and pulled out a large bore flintlock shotgun adorned in the Bedouin style. He claimed it was a gift from his tribe for "the Englishman Lawrence who will crush the Ottomans".

An Arab fighter already in camp who had been awakened by the commotion verified the man's identity.

"He is on our side," said the soldier. "His arm was cut off by the Ottoman pigs."

Isa was given his audience with Lawrence, who sat hidden among other British officers. The Bedouin would have no idea to whom he was presenting the shotgun. Auda Abu Tayi was also there, with his closest aides and bodyguards.

"He presents this famous shotgun to Commander Lawrence," the man who'd recognized Isa earlier translated as Isa knelt and held the gun before him.

"What's so famous about it?" Auda Abu Tayi asked in Arabic.

Isa began to answer, but the interpreter held up his hand. He knew the answer himself, and directed it straight at Lawrence.

"This weapon, praise be to Allah, is famous for killing an Ottoman general and wounding a *pasha* in one single discharge. Isa bin Khalid bin Isa Huwaytati, this man's grandfather, who used the same name, was the one who shot it. He was later hunted down and executed by the Ottomans and members of neighboring tribes."

Convinced, and gripped with a life-long fascination with firearms, T.E. Lawrence was unable to resist an opportunity to inspect the weapon more closely. He stood up from his chair, revealing his identity.

"Let's take a look at this thing," he said, approaching Isa and taking the weapon from him. "Beautiful," Lawrence said, admiring the workmanship, "but unless I get within a few feet of a Turk, or a grouse perhaps, I don't know that this is going to do me much good."

Laughter rang out all around, and even Isa had to smile when he heard the translation.

"No, no," the translator said on Isa's insistence, "this could be very useful. He asks if you have some papers?'"

"Papers?"

The translator paused, listening. "He says 'anything at all. Papers to write on.'"

A small notebook was produced. With a smile and a gleam in his eye—like a magician performing a trick—Isa rolled up the notebook with his hand and inserted the pages into the wide barrel of the shotgun.

"He says you do this with your top-secret papers. If you are about to be overrun, instead of the papers being taken..."

Isa mimed firing the shotgun.

"You blow them to smithereens!" Lawrence exclaimed, finishing the thought for him. "Brilliant! All that classified material gone!"

Everyone laughed again, enjoying the simple ingenuity of the idea.

With much bowing and gratitude on all sides, Isa bin Khalid bin Isa Huwaytati was soon welcomed into the camp and fed a double ration, cementing his tribe's inclusion into the Arab Rebellion.

For the rest of the war, Lawrence was never seen without the handsome weapon at his side, his most secret maps, plans, orders, and documents rolled up inside the barrel.

After the war, Lawrence presented his government-issued Lee-Enfield rifle to King George V. The Bedouin's shotgun was never found.

.

4

Morgantown, WV

Saqqara, Brook's golden retriever, was notoriously disinterested in the various sounds of the ancient Woodburn Hall, situated on the campus of West Virginia University. However, on that particular night, she growled, then barked a sharp rebuke at something she heard out in the hall, startling Brook and causing her to jerk her head painfully off of the soft pillow of term papers she'd been reading before dozing off at her office desk.

"What is it, Saqqara?" Brook asked.

The dog kept growling—a strange, low, frightened sound rumbling from her chest, unlike anything Brook had ever heard from the dog before.

Careful not to make a sound, Brook stood and staggered to the door, wiping her eyes and willing herself awake. She checked her watch—1:00 a.m. She'd often been in the building this late, but it was rare to see anyone else except the janitor, and Saqqara would have recognized him.

"Maybe it's a real ghost this time," Brook suggested out loud, both stalling and summoning added courage. She stood at the door—which had been locked—then opened it.

Saqqara jumped to her feet and barked as she did. Brook feared her dog would charge after whatever was out there and try to kill it. She tensed, ready to grab Saqqara's collar if the dog dashed past.

"Saqqara, heel!" Brook commanded, and the dog obediently stepped up to Brook's left knee as she'd been taught. Brook put her leash on while straining to see what was out in the hall.

It was dark; that much was for sure—the light switch was thirty feet away. A sudden cold gust of air made Brook shiver and the hair on her arms stand on end.

In the darkness, a man brushed past, very close to her side. Brook gasped, Saqqara barked, and suddenly the man was halfway down the hall. He appeared to be around forty years old, dressed in a summer suit with a wide-brimmed hat, his feet clacking against the floor in a pair of shiny oxfords.

Crisp, they'd call him, Brook thought, *like your father.*

As she stared, she realized it *was* her father, the unmistakable Cale Burlington, though he'd been dead ten years.

"Daddy?" Brook questioned in a whisper.

The man kept walking, as if he had business to attend to, mysteries to solve, or crimes to avenge.

It is him! Brook decided, breaking into a run with Saqqara right at her side, still heeling.

He slammed into the door at the end of the hall. It swung shut before Brook burst through it a moment later.

"Daddy!" Brook repeated desperately, the word echoing in the stairwell. He was gone, though the sound of his shoes lingered at a steady pace. She couldn't tell if he was going up or down.

"Which way, Saqqara?" Brook pleaded, but the dog only whimpered, as confused as Brook was.

Down! Brook decided suddenly, leaping down the steps and praying she wouldn't fall. This could be her last chance to say goodbye to him properly…

Sure enough, her feet gave way, and she collapsed on the bottom of the stairwell, leaning against the door to the outside. She began to sob. It couldn't have been her father; it might not have been anyone. She hadn't heard the door open to the outside, and the air here was warm; there'd been no cold gust. She was seeing things; that was all there was to it, or dreaming. It was like something from the Wizard of Oz—"And you were there, and you were there—"

Except her father would never be there. He was dead, and Brook knew exactly where he was buried.

"Go away, you ghosts," she whispered.

Saqqara licked Brook's face, worried for her sanity.

"Have I gone to Heaven?" Brook asked. "Is that why he's here?"

Brook stood. She climbed the stairs to the top floor and looked around, turning on all the lights she could find, checking the men's room, the ladies' room, and the doors of all the locked rooms, like a night-watchman. Campus security came by just once a night— what was there to steal? Books, papers, grades? That was all on computers now anyway. Brook checked the third floor—her floor—followed by the second, and then the first. She saw no one on her way, not even the janitor.

She wondered briefly if he was okay. There was a flu going around.

*   *   *

The phone rang in Carl Burlington's pants pocket. The sound shook Carl awake, and he fumbled around in the darkness trying to find the source. It was probably a wrong number, or somebody selling something. Carl couldn't imagine anything else; his wife was in the bed next to him, the girls were asleep in their room and there'd been no emergency at work—

"Brook?" Carl answered after reading the ID. There was no reply. *A mistake*, Carl hoped. "Brook, did you call me?"

Again, there came no answer, but then he heard it; a slight intake of air, then a gasping sob—loud—excruciating, choking for breath.

"Brook?" he repeated, now worried. She cried while Carl calculated contingency plans and tried to press her for information. "What happened? Are you all right? Where are you? What's wrong?"

Her only answer was sobbing so heart-wrenching that Carl felt himself start to cry along with her. By then, Carl's wife Alicia was awake with her own questions.

"Who is it, Carl? What's wrong? Is someone hurt?"

"Are you at home, Brook?" Carl asked, answering Alicia's first question. "Are you at home? Yes or no?"

"Yes. Home," Brook answered, slurring her speech like someone clinging onto consciousness.

"Are you hurt?" Carl insisted. "Yes or no?"

"No."

Carl's brow furrowed.

"What's wrong, Brook? Tell me what's wrong."

Brook kept crying, but the urgency behind it was gone, which frightened Carl even more. He caught his breath and covered the phone.

"It's my sister," he told Alicia.

"I know," his wife answered. "What's wrong?"

Carl shook his head.

"I'm sorry," Brook babbled through the phone. "I didn't mean to wake you. I didn't know what time it was. I... I don't know anything." She burst into tears again. "Goodbye, Carl."

It sounded final, too final.

"Don't do anything, Brook! Stay where you are and don't do anything!" His pleas were met by a dial tone; Brook had already hung up. Carl stared at his phone in shock. "Redial! Redial!" he yelled as if it would react to voice command, a capability it had never had. Alicia gently took the phone—she was better at this sort of thing than he was.

When the call was put through, Brook didn't answer. Carl jumped out of bed.

"I need to go," he said, scrambling into his clothes.

"Go where?" Alicia asked, incredulous.

"To my sister."

"She's in Morgantown, West Virginia."

"That's right."

"And this is Falls Church, Virginia."

"So?"

"So it's a four-hour drive."

"Three-and-a-half if I push the speed limit."

"That's nuts," Alicia shook her head.

"I have to go to her. You'd want me to go to you if you were in some kind of trouble."

"No," Alicia replied sternly, "I'd want you to call 911." Already, she had her own phone out.

Carl heard the faint voice of an operator as the call connected.

"Falls Church 911. What is your emergency?"

"My sister-in-law just called from Morgantown, West Virginia. Something's wrong, and we need to find out what happened. It sounds like she's in danger."

There was a pause. Both Carl and Alicia expected some sort of bureaucratic nonsense about it being a different city, but instead there was a click and Alicia heard a new voice.

"Morgantown 911. What is your emergency?"

"This is Falls Church 911 requesting a welfare check," the original operator said.

"What is the address?" the operator in Morgantown asked.

"Go ahead, Miss," Alicia heard. Relieved, she read off Brook's address from her contact list.

* * *

For the second time that night, Brook found herself waking to

Saqqara's barking, this time on the hardwood floor of her living room. Her face was wet, and so was the floor. She'd cried herself to sleep, and her phone lay near her head. Red lights were flashing through the front bay windows of her house—the instantly recognizable, whirling, police-car kind. Brook lived in a safe area, and couldn't imagine what would bring the police here. She vaguely remembered having some kind of breakdown, chasing her father through Woodburn Hall, then struggling to drive home—her hands hadn't been working properly and neither had her feet, and her focus and eyesight weren't what they should have been—

Did you hit somebody? Brook wondered, dread filling her stomach. *Have they come to take you away, to charge you with a hit and run or leaving the scene of an accident?*

Filled with crushing guilt, Brook crawled to the front door. Saqqara followed by her side, trying to help somehow. Grabbing the doorknob for support, Brook made it to her feet and looked out of the rectangular window in the door. There were policemen there, but also medics, and an ambulance in the driveway.

* * *

"Mr. Burlington?" the voice on the phone asked.

"Yes. Carl Burlington here," he managed to get out. He was somewhere in Maryland, between Gaithersburg and Germantown, driving eight miles over the limit.

"This is the Morgantown Police Department. We're here with your sister, Brook. She's all right. She's had some sort of breakdown, according to the EMTs, but it's not an emergency situation, so they've gone onto another call—"

"I'm on my way," Carl blurted. "I'll be there in..." Carl checked his watch. "...three hours."

"That's good. We'll have someone stay with her."

"Thank you, thank you so much. May I speak to her?"

"She's been sedated, Mr. Burlington."

"Oh..."

"The medics thought it would be the best."

"I understand."

Carl's head spun as he hung up. He didn't understand; he had no idea.

5

Morgantown, WV

Officially, Brook Burlington was taking a sabbatical from her position at WVU. Not unusual.

"Unofficially," a university spokesman hinted to those who enquired after her with a twinkle in his eye, "she might have embarked on a top-secret mission." The only secret was the one being kept by the University.

A "nervous breakdown" was what Brook had been told had happened, but in her own mind, it was all a blur.

Carl had stayed with Brook that night, helped her pack her things and close up the house, then driven both Brook and Saqqara back with him the next day. Brook, Saqqara and the canopic jar— Brook had insisted it came along—now lived with Carl and his wife and their two children in their comfortable home in Falls Church, near DC. Brook was incredibly grateful to her brother; without him, she wasn't sure what she would have done. She had very few friends, and was desperate not to be a burden. Carl's house had a guest room with its own bath, which Carl claimed they "never used anyway."

Madison and Callie—aged eight and six years old—loved having Aunt Brook around full-time. Carl's wife was also extremely gracious given the circumstances. Alicia worked as a hospital administrator, getting patients in, getting their problems solved, then getting them out as efficiently as possible, and Brook could see her struggling against the urge to treat Brook like another client.

Brook had tried to help out, but after a few days, she came to understand Alicia felt far more comfortable treating Brook as an honored guest rather than a helper around the house. She would settle for guest over patient.

Carl surprised Brook. She hadn't realized what a domestic animal he was. Over the years, he had rarely mentioned Alicia or the girls, and although Brook visited once or twice a year, she had the feeling—unfounded, it turned out—that they weren't his priority. In retrospect, after living among them, Brook realized that Carl was protecting her feelings; recognizing that Brook, being two years older yet without a husband or kids, might not want to hear Carl going on about his familial bliss.

Although they were engaged in a similar pursuit—archaeology—it was Brook who traveled the world and did the digging, literally getting her hands dirty, while Carl stayed at home and acted as administrator for the foundation their father had set up "to further worldwide research in antiquities". Brook had always assumed they were different—she was active, restless, and physical; Carl was cerebral, organized, and calm in a crisis—but she was beginning to see that was a false impression, too. Carl was a family man, and family came first, no matter what his own wishes and desires.

The day of Brook's arrival, Carl had found her a psychiatrist and a general practice physician, and for the first week, Brook's time was filled with appointments and tests, with Carl insisting he drive her to every appointment despite her protestations. She understood the seriousness of her condition; she could see how it worried him, and vowed to be a model patient, even agreeing to a daily dose of an anti-anxiety drug.

"Just to take the edge off until we know what's going on," the doctors had assured her. Unspoken was the threat that if Brook didn't cooperate she'd undoubtedly be sent to an institution "for your own safety and the safety of others".

The worst case scenario, Brook understood, would be if they had a legitimate reason to be worried, and she'd fall back down that same rabbit hole, never to return.

She worried that among the many long legal documents she'd signed was one that had given Carl the right to commit her involuntarily. She desperately wanted to ask, but was also terrified of the answer.

Determined to stabilize, Brook confided to the counselors about her mental and physical exhaustion. She told them she'd seen her father's ghost and was haunted by the image of him, as well as the way he continued to overshadow her success. She told them how isolated and lonely she felt...and about Tom; how seeing him again had made things even more confusing. She summarized a call she had taken directly from the president of the university; there were big plans for the archaeology program, and Brook was expected to take the spotlight.

"We're counting on you to help secure grants and donations to keep everything up and running," he had told her.

"How did that make you feel?" the counselors asked.

"Scared to death," Brook admitted.

"Did you tell him that?"

Brook laughed.

"I promised him I'd get back as soon as possible," she said, shaking her head.

To Carl, Brook only confided that she was thinking of writing a book—*The Story of Cleopatra*. They had discussed it a week or so after Brook moved in while Alicia had been tucking the girls into bed upstairs.

"I want to focus on her as a person," she told her brother, "and Antony—their words, their lives, their sacrifice for love...and Neferu."

Carl looked puzzled for a moment. "The stoneworker?"

"Yes, you remembered," Brook smiled.

"Of course I did, he's the unsung hero. 'The man who saved the Queen—'"

"I don't like the way it's all been sensationalized," Brook stated sadly, cutting him off. "The theft of some of the artifacts. Russian mobsters. American speculators..." Brook shook her head. Other books had already come out and been instant best sellers, thrillers 'based on a true story'. Brook had been asked to read a dozen of them, mostly to write glowing forewords or provide endorsements. She'd turned down every request, handing the books themselves to her grad students, who enjoyed making fun of them in drunken late-night reveries.

"So, do you wanna come down to the Burlington Foundation tomorrow?" Carl asked cheerfully, sensing Brook's downturn in mood.

"Sure..." Brook answered hesitantly. "What for?"

"To work, of course," Carl replied. "You'd have to volunteer, but our need is great and your skill is legendary. And, of course, the work experience might pad your resume," he laughed.

"Okay, cut it out. I'll come, but no promises. One day."

"That's all I ask."

"One day at a time."

"Exactly."

"How is the Foundation doing, anyway?" Brook asked, suddenly excited to be talking about something besides Cleopatra, Antony, or her own mental state.

"Busy, busy, busy," Carl told her.

"Still tracking stolen Iraqi material?"

"You bet," Carl affirmed. "We've got thousands of artifacts and millions of leads. If ISIS didn't loot the stuff, somebody else did. Iraq, Syria, Afghanistan——it's now moving east *and* west. It's heading to Europe and Russia, and more and more, the Chinese are getting a taste. You'd think they'd have enough of their own antiquities."

"Do you have people in the field?" Brook inquired, a sudden

idea popping into her head.

Carl, realizing where her thoughts were headed, shook his finger.

"No, no, no," he said. "We're fully covered on that score. I don't need you traipsing all over the world like you're chasing down Carmen Sandiego We've got Sam Spade, Poirot, Sherlock Holmes *and* Miss Marple looking into things on four continents, and Interpol and the United Nations are at our disposal. You're grounded right here for a while."

"Oh well. It was just a thought."

"Well, don't think," Carl sighed. "Not right now."

It sounded sterner than Carl meant, Brook could tell, but for now she said nothing, and would continue to say nothing. It wasn't in her nature to stay quiet, but Brook suspected she was on thin ice. She'd noticed earlier that evening how Alicia always managed to make sure she was never alone with Madison and Callie, which both angered and saddened her, yet again she would say nothing.

Tell it to the shrink, Brook told herself, before she gave her head a quick shake. *No, don't. She'll think you're paranoid and lock you up.*

"I know you don't want me to mention this again..." Carl began as they drove to the foundation the next morning.

"I know—Mom."

"She called again yesterday," Carl said with a sigh.

"Why does she call you? She has my number."

"She's trying to be sensitive."

"Mom? Sensitive? Don't make me laugh." Brook said flatly.

"She just wants you to come up and see her, and finally meet her new husband—what's-his-name—"

"Albert," she interjected.

"You missed the wedding."

"I was on a dig."

"*Which* you arranged so you wouldn't have to go to the wedding," Carl accused. Brook didn't deny it. "Anyway, that was two years ago," he added.

"I'm sick," she told him. "Mentally unbalanced. I couldn't stand the pressure."

Carl glanced over—was Brook kidding?

"Is that what you want me to tell Mom?" he asked. "You're insane, and seeing her again would put you over the edge?"

Brook didn't answer for a moment.

"Tell her anything you want, since you and her and what's-his-name are such good friends."

"Albert," Carl filled in.

"Albert," Brook repeated.

*   *   *

The Foundation was as busy as advertised, with half a dozen employees and several volunteer interns from a couple of nearby colleges bustling around the offices. To Brook's embarrassment, her impending arrival had been announced earlier, and she was given the red-carpet treatment by the staff, some of whom she'd known for many years, but hadn't seen since the discovery of Cleopatra.

The scene was further enhanced by her gift of the canopic jar, which was to be placed in a display case at the Foundation's small museum.

"This way the jar will be covered under our insurance," Carl had assured her.

The staff had a million questions for Brook, and she tried her best to be present and answer every one. On one hand, she hated the attention, but on the other, she was grateful Carl hadn't instructed his staff to treat her like a fragile valuable. When it came to the jar, however, Brook had to admit she knew absolutely nothing about it, or its sender.

"Okay, that's enough," Carl told the gathered crowd when he realized Brook was becoming exhausted. "We need to get back to work here."

"Thank you, all of you," Brook told the group as they dispersed.

Carl showed Brook to an office, pointing out the small day bed along one wall.

"You're welcome to take a nap anytime you like," he said.

"Thanks," she answered. Now the crowds had dispersed, she was back to being treated with kid gloves. She had hoped that helping at the Foundation would change the way Carl dealt with her, but it clearly made no difference. "Maybe later."

"Okay let me show you what we're up against," Carl said, booting up the computer on the desk.

It was a daunting task Carl had taken on almost single-handedly. The Islamic State, in addition to all its other ventures, were selling licenses to local thieves to steal from existing museums, sites, and digs, then forcing the same thieves to sell their stolen wares to ISIS itself as cheaply as possible. No site was spared, and no artifact passed by. Bibles, statues, cuneiform tablets, cylinder seals, and even canopic jars had been taken from the ground, standing sites, and numerous museums throughout conflict zones.

"So in the beginning, there is 'The List,'" Carl intoned, pulling up a five hundred-page spreadsheet, "This contains details of every artifact that is known or rumored to have been lost in a war or plundered by thieves. "

"Oh my," Brook gasped under her breath.

"Yeah," Carl agreed. "It's not digging like you're used to, but it's digging nevertheless."

"Are the Cleopatra artifacts—?"

"No, none of them. We're staying away from those completely, and so should you."

Brook nodded. The entire experience was a source of anxiety and shame for her, and she was almost glad to be separate from it for once.

A polite cough from Carl brought her thoughts back to the task at hand.

Important artifacts are missing—focus!

He showed her links to photographs of each object, along with a confirmation or best guess as to where the objects were now. He sat back and cleared his throat:

"So yeah, that's the job. Keeping the list. It's vital. We've used catalogs from museums, pre-war brochures from the tourist destinations, academic papers, National Geographic Specials, books, memories, anything we can get hold of to tell us what was there before..."

"Then you gotta figure out where it all went," Brook finished.

"That's it."

"And get it back to the rightful owner?"

"Well, that's the ultimate goal," Carl agreed, "but that's probably decades off, and there's no point sending these priceless relics back into harm's way."

"No…" Brook paused.

"Take whatever time you need," Carl told her. "It would be such a help."

Brook didn't know about that. It was basically clerical work; something she didn't feel she was much good at and that bored her to tears. What they really needed was a librarian, or a statistician— so what if she knew a little something about what she was looking at? That part of it didn't matter, really, the artifacts were simply widgets at this point, or words in boxes, and whether those words described items assumed lost three thousand years ago or last week didn't make much difference.

"At first it seems insurmountable," Carl confessed while they ate lunch in his office that afternoon, "but then you start to see patterns. Stuff purloined on one day in one spot all tends to get bought by a single buyer halfway around the world."

"So who makes the inquiries? Who sends the emails and makes the phone calls?" Brook asked.

"We all do. It depends on who we're calling, and who anybody here already knows and has a relationship with."

"What about Alicia? Does she send emails and make phone calls for you?" Brook asked, gauging Carl's reaction to the mention of his wife.

"Well, yes. She's helped out from time to time," he said calmly, revealing nothing.

"Like last week, and the week before that?" Brook suggested.

"Nights and weekends. She has a full-time job—"

"I don't want to take your wife's job here, Carl. I won't."

"You're not. As I said, she works full time. She has the girls, too."

"Carl, no. This isn't right. If you two want to work together—"

"Okay, okay. It was just an idea."

Brook went quiet for a moment, picking at her food. "What's Redtail?"

Carl froze, a forkful of salad halfway to his face.

"Redtail?" he half whispered, half choked.

"That's right."

"Let's go," Carl said, putting down his fork, and escorting Brook out of the office, then out the building. He pointed to the highway. "Walk."

Next to the traffic, the noise was deafening, which was exactly what Carl wanted, Brook realized. It was clear he was disturbed by her question, angry even, but she had no idea why. She mused about the trash they were walking through next to the road, wondering what a civilization a thousand years in the future would make of the candy wrappers, soda bottles, used condoms and diapers strewn everywhere. Much of Brook's life had been spent sifting through the tossed out remains of past civilizations, and considerations of how her own civilization would present itself to the archeologists of the future were difficult to switch off.

"You have to forget about Redtail," Carl told Brook over the roar of the highway. He held his hand over his mouth when he spoke, like he was leading a conference on the mound at a baseball game, and his eyes scanned the area. "Alicia screwed up—that shouldn't have appeared on your computer. She figured she was coming back, then I sprung you on her—"

"What's it about?" Brook asked, covering her mouth the same way Carl did. She figured he might be as crazy as she was at this point, but the fear on his face was no delusion.

"You don't have clearance," Carl answered flatly.

"Does *Alicia* have clearance?" Brook asked, incredulous.

"Yes, she does."

"She works in a hospital!"

"This is Washington, DC."

"This is Falls Church, Virginia!" Brook argued.

"Twenty-minute drive, right down there," Carl said, pointing down the highway. He was pointing the wrong way, but Brook didn't correct him. "Government officials come to Alicia's hospital, they go under anesthesia, they get operations, and they lay around in recovery, talking in their sleep, no doubt."

"Spies, you mean. NSA? CIA?"

"Yeah, and Senators and Congresspeople; they know things. Even their presence in the hospital could be a State secret, so she has clearance."

"And so do you."

Carl nodded, then shrugged.

"Crazy, isn't it?" he said. "After the reputation our dad had. I mean, Alicia and I don't have access to the *top* top secret, like the nuclear codes or anything, but stuff below that..." he trailed off, eying her warily. "They might even take that away now that I've let you in the building, Brook."

"Oh, come on." She rolled her eyes.

"You just had a nervous breakdown," Carl pointed out.

"Yeah, okay," she answered sarcastically, cutting him off before she got really angry. "I'm your *sister*, Carl!"

Carl took the hit, but it looked like he still wouldn't say anything.

"Redtail?" she pressed.

"Okay," he replied, "but this is all I will say about it, and then you need to forget it."

"Sure."

"When an artifact says 'Redtail'," Carl said slowly, "it means its recovery has taken a different—and very specific—route. Generally, it means the foundation—*our* foundation—has purchased it back from a jihadist group."

"The foundation does that? We have *the money* for that?"

Carl shook his head.

"No, but the US government does. They're acting on behalf of other nations, either out of goodwill or to extract something from someone, I don't know. It's all above my pay-grade, but just to find out what the relics are and who has them involves intelligence. That's where the spies come in. People are risking their lives to get these treasures back, so we buy the material on behalf of the government. If the jihadists thought Uncle Sam was the buyer, the price would go sky-high, and if the American people knew that their hard-earned tax dollars were being handed over to some of our biggest enemies, well...you fill in the rest."

"Chaos. All for a bunch of clay pots and a bronze plate or two," Brook finished. "Okay, you're forgiven. Let's go back—it's cold out here."

Against Carl's objections, and at her insistence, instead of returning to the computer, Brook spent the rest of the day going through her father's material in a basement room of the foundation's offices.

"It's all junk," Carl complained as he showed her in. "It's not worth your time."

"It's our family legacy," Brook said brightly. "And I need to dig through *something* or I'm just gonna die!"

Carl laughed and left the room.

Brook wasn't sure her father would appreciate his legacy sharing space in the basement with the water heater, air conditioner, forgotten file cabinets, and various computers, printers, shredders and other electronics which may or may not have worked but that no one had the time to go through and dispose of in a responsible manner.

In spite of that, Brook loved it down there. For once, she was alone. She'd forgotten how much she enjoyed "alone time," though suddenly, for the first time, she missed Saqqara. The girls' allergy to dogs had forced Brook to call her friend Katy, who had driven to Carl's house, collected the dog, and promised to house-sit Brook's place for, "as long as it takes." Katy had also offered to take care of Brook, for which she was eternally grateful.

Brook reached into the mountain of Cale Burlington material, picked something out, and sank to the concrete floor. She held a beat-up case file made of leather, as old school as you got. Blowing off a layer of dust, Brook ran her fingers along the gold lettering embossed on the jacket, "Cale's Stuff". Smiling, Brook opened the book.

6

Falls Church, VA

"I'm going to see Mom," Brook announced the next morning to Carl, Alicia, and the girls at the breakfast table.

"What?" Carl exclaimed, clearly taken aback after her repeated refusals to do just that.

"I'm going to see Mom. I called her this morning—she and Albert get up at the crack of dawn, apparently, and go walking every day. She was thrilled, of course, and said to come right over, so I called for a car rental, and they're coming to pick me up—"

The quick honk of a car horn interrupted Brook's energetic monologue.

"—now," Brook concluded. "I'll be back later tonight.; I can't imagine I'll stay over. You know there's only so much family I can take! "

Without another word, Brook was out the door, leaving everyone at the breakfast table to look at each other with stunned stares. Carl noted the items she'd taken with her—her own leather messenger case and an ancient leather-bound case file she'd dredged up from the basement of the foundation.

Alicia looked to him for some explanation.

Carl shrugged—he didn't have one.

*   *   *

It was nice to be driving again; Brook had to admit. Her mother Rose lived an hour or so away, in Lake Shore, Maryland, just south of Baltimore. Her new husband, Albert, worked for the IRS—or used to, Brook wasn't sure. Regardless, he had to be close to DC, but didn't drive in every day, or something like that. Brook hadn't paid much attention.

"Happy-go-lucky" was what others said about Brook's mother, but Brook always stuck with "flighty". In Brook's mind, her mother always managed to say the wrong thing. It was obvious that Rose wanted her to be a girly-girl, and would have preferred that at least one of her offspring *not* take up their father's profession. There'd been pressure for Brook to get married and have children, too, "just like Carl".

She was stuck in Washington traffic going into the city, and would probably hit traffic going out on the Maryland side, then the Baltimore traffic.

"Should have gone via the Beltway," she said, talking to herself. "Bethesda, Silver Spring, Chevy Chase." Brook didn't know the Washington area that well, but she knew that.

According to Carl, Albert was the polar opposite of Cale.

"Dispassionate, a homebody, nerdy, and frail," was how Carl had described him.

"Wow, what a catch," Brook had responded. "Mom went to the other end of the spectrum this time, huh?"

"Right."

Alone in the rental car, Brook put it all out of her mind—she would find out soon enough what the deal with Albert was.

She turned on the radio and sang along with Ozzy Osbourne: "Times have changed and times are strange, here I come, but I ain't the same...Mama, I'm coming home."

* * *

Rose and Albert greeted Brook warmly on the porch of their lovely-but-modest home. Albert hung back while Rose and Brook engaged in a marathon catch-up session in the living room. To Brook's relief, her mother seemed to know nothing about her recent breakdown, and Brook didn't feel the need to share. If Rose was avoiding mentioning it out of politeness—which was completely within her character—Brook wouldn't stop her.

Albert made them all lunch once the two women were up to speed.

"Isn't he a wonderful cook?" Rose gushed. Brook fought the urge to roll her eyes.

"For a wonderful person," Albert gushed right back.

They kissed, as if demonstrating their affection to Brook. She made a mental note to tell Carl later.

"Mom, I wondered if I could go through Dad's old stuff," she broached once the meal was over and Albert had cleared the table.

"Oh," Rose answered, obviously disappointed. *That's why you came,* her crestfallen expression suggested.

Brook placed her hand on Rose's. "It's important to me."

"I understand. You're like your father. I get it." The tightness in her voice suggested she was angry, but she'd never express it openly.

"Mom..."

"All that junk is up in the attic," Rose answered crisply. "It's not doing us any good here—if it helps you, you're welcome to it."

"Thank you."

"I'll show you how to get up there," she told her daughter, pushing back from the table. "This way."

The attic was half-filled with Albert's things from a previous marriage. Whether his wife had died or he was divorced, Brook didn't know—or had forgotten. As she picked her way to the Burlington side of the attic, she wondered if there was some way to tactfully find out. She had a lot of questions, actually, but knew she should have asked them years ago.

Examining the pile of things she had to search through, Brook kicked herself—she should have rented a van, taken all her father's materials back to the foundation, and wouldn't have needed to return. She felt guilty about dragging everything back up for her mother like this, but knew it needed to be done

You gotta do what you gotta do, Brook told herself. *Then tell the shrink, right? Isn't that the way this works?*

She could bring Carl back with her when she returned—the attic was accessed via a rickety ladder and a hole in the ceiling, making it hard for one person to carry much on their own—and get it all done in one day. She'd make it a bit of a family reunion;

the best kind, when there was a task at hand and not too much down time to dredge up old issues.

"Down to business," Brook stated, slapping her hands together like some sort of cartoon character. She cleared an empty area in one section of the attic and began moving items from Cale's life into it one piece at a time.

She was looking for something very specific; a shotgun matching the description of one noted in the leather case-file at the foundation. The file indicated the shotgun had been found in a lost cache near Petra. Arabs had stashed it on Lawrence's behalf ahead of the Third Battle of Gaza as they carried out an operation to divert Ottoman forces. None of those Arabs were available to retrieve the cache; some were killed in the operation, others simply went home.

Brook was intrigued by the story—*Treasure Island* came to mind—and she was certain her father must have been just as fascinated. He would want to locate and obtain an item like that; one that came with a story and upon which history had hinged.

A packet disintegrated in Brook's hand, and photographs fell to the dusty floor. She dropped to pick them up, and quickly found herself weeping. The photos were of her father—young, grinning, and full of life—holding up artifacts, one after another, on Greek isles, Mediterranean beaches, and Middle Eastern ruins. There were pictures of her with him, too—the two desperate in their love for each other, peas in a pod. It had been a long time since Brook had seen these photos.

"Are you all right?" Rose asked, her head popping up through the square hole in the attic, like a jack-in-the-box.

"I'm fine," Brook sobbed. She suddenly realized her mother must have taken these pictures. Rose had captured the special bond between father and daughter over and over without complaint, and for the most part, Rose was not pictured in any of them.

"I found these, that's all," she sniffled, grabbing a handful of the photos and taking them to her mother. Rose did not cry, but her expression changed as she flicked through the pictures, and it was clear she was also deeply moved.

"He was the love of my life," she whispered to Brook. "Love of my life...scared the hell out of me, too."

Brook blubbered a laugh.

"Like you," Rose said quietly. It was all the emotion she could handle. She put the photos down carefully and respectfully and climbed back down the ladder, her hands shaking. Whether it was from old age or emotion, Brook couldn't tell.

Once her mother had left, Brook fell on her back, stared at the rafters, and made no attempt to control her tears.

"You're lucky," she was sure her psychiatrist would tell her later. "Some girls hate their fathers...and their mothers."

Brook rolled over, found a shoebox amid the discarded rubble, and placed the photographs into it. She'd take them back now, at least.

Her eyes widened as something caught her eye. There it was she was certain of it! A case—actually, more of a crate—hand-made and crudely aged by hot weather and cold hearts.

It's just the right size for a dozen long-stemmed roses...or a shotgun!

Throwing all organization aside, Brook shoved away the mountain of material stacked up in front of it. When she picked it up, she wasn't disappointed; it was exactly the right weight. She wanted to open it right then and there, but it had been screwed shut—not nailed, screwed! Only a valuable object would be stored this way.

She pushed it next to the hole in the ceiling and crawled down ahead of it. As many priceless relics as she'd dug up from the ground, this was the first time Brook had pulled something *down*.

"Mom!" Brook called after wrangling the heavy, awkward case out of the attic. She took it out to the back deck. As wonderful as Brook hoped its contents would be, she was sane enough to realize it was also a filthy hunk of wood slats, dust, and possible termites.

Rose and Albert rushed out to the back deck.

"Screwdriver. Screwdriver," she huffed, out of breath from exertion and excitement.

At least Albert was calm. He checked which tool would be needed—flathead or Phillips—and returned shortly with two screwdrivers of exactly the right size and type. He and Brook attacked the dozen screws on the lid.

"Save the screws," Brook ordered. "They might be important."

Rose went inside and brought back a plastic sandwich bag.

After the screws were removed with a little prying, the lid came off. Carefully, Brook pulled off layers of newspaper wrapping—written in Arabic, she noticed—putting them aside in a pile. Where and when the papers came from might be important later.

Then it was there, in front of their eyes: the shotgun!

"A gift from Isa bin Khalid bin Isa Huwaytati to T.E. Lawrence, if I'm not mistaken." Brook announced.

"Lawrence of Arabia?" Albert asked from over her shoulder.

"That's right. Let's see..."

Brook reached down and picked up the weapon.

"Careful, it might still be loaded," Albert warned, extending his hands out, silently offering to take it.

Reluctantly, Brook placed the gun in his hands.

"My dad used to take me duck hunting," he explained as he studied the weapon. "This one would kill a whole flock. Look how wide the diameter of the barrel is. It's a beauty, all right, and should operate on a pretty straightforward pump-action, I think. Excuse me."

Albert walked ten feet into the backyard, put the gun to his shoulder, and pointed it into the air. He grasped the pump under the barrel and jerked it back with all his strength. The chamber popped open, and a round popped out. He pumped it a few more times, but that was the only one inside. After gently putting the gun down, Albert picked up the shell, impressed at its size.

"Just one round in there. Modeled after the Winchester 1897, but with a much bigger bore. No idea what you'd need that for."

"Maybe I'll show you," Brook answered, taking the shotgun back. She turned it on herself, making her mother gasp, and moved to where the sun hit it just right—

There it was, inside the barrel! A document—documents?

"See?" Brook showed Albert.

"Well, I'll be," he said incredulously. "A burn box!"

"That's right," Brook laughed. "Spoken like a real IRS agent."

7

Falls Church, VA

"Who do you have on your team who's good with documents?" Brook demanded as she stormed into Carl's house that evening with the shotgun crate tucked under her arm.

"Good with documents, how? Translations?"

"No, restorations. Handling, rubber gloves stuff—"

"We do have someone..." he told Brook. He and Alicia had been watching the late news in the living room. Alicia muted the sound.

"Can you get them to the foundation in the morning?" Brook asked.

Carl checked his watch.

"I guess it's not too late to call. What's this about?"

Brook put the crate on the floor and opened it easily; duct tape now replaced the screws and bubble wrap replaced the newspapers. She carefully pulled out the shotgun .

"Whoa!" Carl exclaimed, holding his hands up instinctively.

"That's not loaded, is it?"

"Not anymore."

"Where'd you get that?"

"Dad's stuff in the attic."

"Wow."

"It's was given to T.E. Lawrence by a prominent tribesman during the Turkish campaign," Brook explained.

"Wow," Carl repeated.

"But that's not the important thing," Brook told her brother. She tipped the gun up under the floor lamp and signaled him over to look down the barrel. "You, too, Alicia. You've got to see this."

All three of them tried to look down it at once without bumping heads.

"You're absolutely certain this isn't loaded?" Carl repeated.

"C'mon, Carl, live a little," Brook joked. She hadn't felt this good since discovering Cleopatra's mummy.

"Whoa," he said, spotting the documents rolled up into the barrel of the shotgun.

"See?" Brook said. "It's a burn box."

"What's that?" Carl asked.

"Like a paper-shredder!" Alicia laughed, getting it.

"What?"

"You fire the gun, Carl," Alicia told him, "and anything in the barrel either gets shredded or burnt up, I don't know which. We'd have to try it to find out."

"Some other time," Brook laughed, pulling the weapon away from her brother and his wife. "I have a feeling that the papers in there must be very important to deserve this kind of security."

"That's why you need a document tech!" Carl understood, pulling his phone from his pocket. "You don't want to be trying to pull that out with a pair of tweezers."

He walked away, dialing, to speak privately with his specialist on the other end of the line. Brook and Alicia heard him make contact, and Alicia turned to her sister-in-law.

"How did it go?" she asked quietly.

"Fantastic," Brook answered, holding up the shotgun.

"I meant with your mother and her new husband..."

"They're great," Brook said sincerely. "I mean, he's not my dad, but he seems to love Mom and takes care of her...and she..." Brook trailed off, not sure what to say next. "He's a good guy, really. Much better than I had made him out to be. I thought..." Again, Brook couldn't go on.

"You thought what?" Alicia asked.

"I thought she just married him because she hated my dad and everything about him...all the stuff that was like me. But that's not it. Maybe she married him to get over Dad at first, but now...it's fine. It's really all fine."

"I'm so glad," Alicia replied honestly.

Brook turned away, quickly wiping a tear away so Carl wouldn't see it as he strolled back into the room, pleased with his accomplishment.

"Tanisha will be there at nine in the morning, gloves and all—" he stopped short, suddenly aware of something going on between the two women. "What?"

"That's great," Brook said, turning back with a forced smile. "I better get to sleep. Tomorrow's a big day."

With that, she put the shotgun back in the case and took it to the guest room, hiding it under her bed.

*   *   *

The old Brook would have been amazed by the potential discovery of an artifact that could help shine a light on otherwise unknown world history, but the new Brook was dismayed beyond all suffering. Gone were her dreams of drifting back into academic oblivion. She knew the documents inside the shotgun barrel would be explosive even if she never actually had to pull the trigger, and their ramifications would certainly cause a stir one hundred years after they were drawn up. Wars could be fought and people might die, all because of the contents of the gun-barrel.

"Maybe that's why Dad never made his findings public," Brook suggested. "Maybe he just stuffed the pages back in the gun and said, 'I can't deal with this.'"

"That's what you're thinking of doing, isn't it?" Carl asked.

They were walking again, back by the highway, where they hoped no one would be able to listen in on their conversation.

"Dad never shied from the limelight," he observed.

"No, but this..."

"Tell me again. Go slow. I'm not sure I understand,"

"Okay," Brook began, taking a deep breath. "The woman you hired—what's her name?"

"Tanisha."

"Yeah, Tanisha. She's terrific, by the way—"

"You're stalling."

"I'm scared to death, okay?"

"Okay, take it easy." Carl tried to keep his tone light, but it sounded condescending.

Brook sighed. If she was right, this would just be the beginning. *The first day in Hell*, she thought darkly.

"Tanisha got the papers out in terrific shape, and she smoothed out and stabilized the newspapers the gun was wrapped in as well," Brook explained. "They're the real deal—newspapers in Arabic from Amman, Jordan, at about the time Dad would have found the shotgun. If my theory is right, Dad found it along with a cache of World War I material near Petra."

"That would sync up with the newspapers," Carl reasoned.

"Right. And it aligns with the case file that got me started on this crazy thing," Brook added bitterly. He was about to respond, but she cut him off. "I'm okay. I'll tell you what I know and keep my feelings out of it."

Carl waited.

Brook sighed again. "The shotgun was found near Petra alongside a large trunk, and was situated near a great deal of military hardware circa 1917-1919, presumably used during the Arab uprising against the Ottoman Turks. The trunk was labeled T.E.L."

"Lawrence of Arabia," Carl realized, nearly releasing a whistle.

"That's what Dad says in his notes. Anyway, the important thing..."

"Is the documents in the gun," he pressed.

"A tentative agreement between the British and the Kurds promising a free and autonomous Kurdistan in exchange for their support fighting against the Ottomans. It was secret. Top secret. And written a year after the Sykes Picot Agreement."

"Refresh my memory," Carl said.

"Sykes Picot was the secret deal the British and French made with each other to slice up and divide the Middle East between the two. It was made public and basically enacted after World War I was over except for the inclusion of one region, Kurdistan."

"Which still doesn't exist," Carl observed.

"No, it doesn't. Even now, one hundred years later. But the contract was signed, the treaty made—"

"It's breach of contract," Carl interrupted. "It's not any of our business. Our business is to explore the past."

"No matter how many people get killed as a result?" Brook asked.

Carl thought about that.

"Besides," Brook added, "I don't know if I can handle the pressure of the fallout."

Carl took a long look at his sister.

"Are you sure about the accuracy of what you're saying?" he asked.

"Enough to be alarmed."

"Your Arabic is good enough to read the document?"

"There are three copies: Arabic, English, and Kurdish. I can read enough of the Arabic to see it matches the English. I think we should assume the Kurdish is the same, since it's the same length."

"I'll find a translator."

"No!" Brook insisted angrily. "If you get a Kurd here to translate and they realize what they're reading, let alone the importance of it, they'll tell the world. Then all hell breaks loose and we're right in the middle of it. And it's not a treaty, it's an agreement. A deal-memo, or list of demands agreed to and checked off. Bullet-points, the kind of thing you'd write up on a cocktail napkin."

"Not a formal treaty?"

"Not even close," she admitted. "But I know there is one. I can feel it in my bones. Dad said there was one in his notes. He exaggerated things, but I don't think he'd lie about that. I need to find it."

Carl nodded. Once she had her mind on something, Brook wouldn't let it go, and he knew she was right about what a powder keg this was.

"Brook, you remember that when we were kids we'd go out in the woods?"

"Yeah," Brook answered with an abundance of patience despite her annoyance at the sudden change of subject.

"You'd lift up every rock to see what kind of spiders, snakes, and bugs were crawling under there."

"I remember," Brook chuckled. "You warned me not to do that or else I'd get bit and die."

"Uh-huh."

"It hasn't happened yet, Carl. Not yet."

They walked back to the foundation. Brook knew that Carl's

story had given her just enough courage to see what would happen when she lifted up a much bigger rock.

*   *   *

For the first time in her professional life, Brook found research exciting. She was stuck in front of computer screen, sure, but her task, as she saw it, was thrilling. She needed to authenticate the documents she'd found inside the shotgun, as well as the shotgun itself, and then piece together those objects' place in history. A big challenge to the project was the fact that even after 100 years, the Kurds' position in the Middle East had never been settled.

The Turkish government considered them terrorists; the Iraqis had a long history of discrimination—and indeed outright genocide—against them, and the Syrians wanted them wiped out, too. Through it all, the Kurds persisted, and as hated as they were by some in the region, they were strong allies for the United States, NATO, and other world powers in the fight against jihadist extremists. The Kurds were fierce fighters who—like the Jews, the Palestinians, the Armenians, the Yazidi, the Tutsi, and so many others before them—had refused to be expunged from history. A treaty guaranteeing them a homeland, no matter how old it was or how much it might seem to some to be a moot point, was dynamite in the most volatile part of the world, and Brook would need to work in complete secrecy.

And then there was the other factor...

Brook's mind drifted back to her childhood, and the night that started it all. She was eight, and they had lived near Washington. Her father had found a part-time lectureship at Georgetown. It was the low point in Cale's career, no doubt, but Brook cherished that time he was at home.

Rose and Cale had been thrilled to see the man who had turned up on their doorstep, brought in a black limousine—Brook remembered that much. His name was Jacob Linksy, and to Brook he seemed to be all beard and wool, like Santa Claus. His glasses were thick, hanging precariously on his face, and he looked a little stunned as her parents danced around him. There was much hugging, kissing, and, eventually, drinking.

Later, long before she became an archaeologist in her own right, Brook had learned exactly what all the excitement was about. Jacob Linsky came with the information her father had been yearning for all his life, linking the ancients of the Old World to the ancients of the New World, to Polynesia and the East.

Petra was the key to it all. In the south of what was now Jordan, it had been the crossroads between Europe and the East, Russia and Africa, and the Mediterranean and the world.

Brook had kept the drawing Linsky made on a sheet of paper that night, full of crisscrossing lines between Zimbabwe and the Mediterranean, Sinai and Petra, from the Persian Gulf to India, over the Bay of Bengal to Cambodia, on to the Philippines, Papeete, and Latin America.

It was compelling stuff, red meat dangled in front of a lion of a man—Cale Burlington, Brook's father—who was hungry after all the letdowns.

Too bad Jacob Linsky's story had all been a hoax. Fake. A scam. The ultimate betrayal, part of a ploy to get Cale to Petra in order to legitimatize what had turned out to be a massive looting operation to steal antiquities and smuggle them to the far corners of the Earth.

Linsky and his allies had played Cale like a fiddle, stroking his ego, playing to his academic biases, catching him at a particularly vulnerable point in his life.

"What do you think, Dad?" Brook asked the computer screen. "Is this shotgun the real deal or just part of the baloney they were feeding you?"

The first thing Brook was sure of was that her father had believed the legend he'd written down in his notes—that a Bedouin had entered Lawrence's camp, given him the weapon, and explained its history—but her father's belief didn't make it true. It was just the kind of romanticized idea they had been baiting him with all those years ago. Thinking back, Brook couldn't ever remember her father being skeptical about *anything* Linsky had told him.

"Naïve. However, on the plus side," Brook muttered to herself, drawing a line through a sheet of paper, "Lawrence is known to have hidden out in the ruins of Petra."

As a trained and experienced archaeologist, Lawrence would have marveled at the spectacular remnants of long-lost civilizations. It was from those ruins, Brook knew, that he launched many of his attacks on the Turks. If her father had in fact uncovered the shotgun and documents with other T.E. Lawrence material in Petra, as he said—

"Well, that does make sense," Brook concluded aloud, writing 'Petra' on the side of the ledger.

Now about this agreement with the Kurds...

On that, too, all Brook had was her father's notes. She made a call.

"Maxwell?"

"Hey, Brook! How are you? *Where* are you? Escaped in the middle of the night, I hear. Tell me where and I'll join you. I'm begging, Brook. Please!"

Brook laughed.

"Sorry, Maxwell, only room for one here, and it's not that exciting, believe me," Brook replied. "Listen, I need some shorthand on World War I, T.E. Lawrence, and the Kurds."

"Ah, okay," he answered, thinking. He was in the History Department, a specialist in the 19th and 20th century. "Nothing old enough for you, dear," he'd once told Brook.

"It's interesting stuff, actually. The English and the French carved up the Middle East even before World War I was over, which Lawrence found appalling but couldn't do much about. The Kurds were intended to be part of that deal—penciled in to get their own country at the end of it. In the end, the Turks balked at the idea, and Europe just claimed what they wanted. The Kurds got a raw deal and they're still paying for it. Does that help you at all?"

"Yes, it confirms what I thought. I've got some names..." Brook proceeded to list a few Arab and British notables who her father had identified as being instrumental to the treaty that followed what Brook had found. The final name on the list—a

Major Edward William Charles Noel—had actually signed the document hidden inside the gun, along with Lawrence and an indecipherable scrawl described as the "Ambassador to Kurdistan".

Maxwell hummed thoughtfully. "I'd have to do a little research to tell you anything helpful."

"But you've heard of these people?"

"Oh, yes, all of them. Edward Noel was a well-known British officer and spy involved in India and the Middle East. He was also an associate of Lawrence's. They were up to all sorts of things together, apparently. I'm not sure about what happened to the Major, though, I think he was a Colonel by the end. What's this all about?"

"I don't know yet, Maxwell," Brook replied. "But keep it under your hat, will you?"

"Ooh, secrets and scandals," Maxwell joked. "Who am I going to tell?"

They said goodbye and hung up, and Brook turned her attention back to the original document. The language used was interesting—the Arab and British signatories promised to recognize the government of a free Kurdistan, and pledged financial and material support to "whatever territory the Kurds conquered". There was no delineation of their territory; and they were seemingly being spurred on by the other powers to take as much as they could hold.

8

"It's not you. It has nothing to do with you. You and Alicia have been wonderful," Brook told Carl. "I need to get away, that's all. Not from you, from the whole thing. I need to get back to work—the kind of work *I* do; being on-site, digging, getting my hands dirty. I admire what you do, Carl, but it isn't for me."

"You had a breakdown, Brook."

"I know that. And it could happen again—"

"In some remote outpost where there'd be no way to get help," Carl argued.

"That's a chance I'll have to take," Brook admitted, "but I really think if I'm out there doing what I do without the stress of being famous or people clawing at me..."

She didn't finish. She could see Carl wasn't buying it.

"You haven't given this half a chance, Brook," Carl said softly. "It's been what, ten days since you came across the papers and the shotgun? You've barely scratched the surface as far as research; you don't even really understand the basic history yet. You need to explore the library before the entire country of Jordan."

"Carl, that's not me."

"What does your therapist say about this?" he asked.

"She agrees with me. She thinks it's a good idea."

He grunted.

"I think we should find someone else," he said.

Brook laughed, but her brother's expression didn't soften.

"I'm not kidding," he said. "I think you should get a second opinion."

"The second and last opinion is mine," Brook said, gauging Carl's reaction. If he had a trump card—like Power of Attorney over her—now would be the time to play it, to tell her that as her legal guardian, overseer of her estate, or whatever he might be, he wouldn't allow it.

"What about the foundation?" Carl asked instead. "This is just going to get us into trouble. It's explosive international politics you're playing with here, Brook. What if it all comes out, our relationships..." Carl trailed off. They were in his office, not down by the highway. If the place was bugged, he didn't want to say too much.

"I'll be discreet," Brook said in a whisper.

"If it all goes south, Dad's name will come up again."

"It hasn't yet. I've been interviewed a hundred times, and it's always 'daughter of famed archaeologist Cale Burlington.' He's never a 'disgraced archaeologist,' and besides, the foundation's association with me hasn't been so bad up to now, has it? I remember what a sleepy, nothing-burger place this was before Cleopatra."

Carl didn't reply. He wouldn't win this argument, and it wouldn't do to make Brook angry. They'd had their differences, but Brook had the ability to freeze him out, and he didn't want that. He couldn't stop her, but he was worried.

"What if it's just another scam?" he asked intensely. "Or part of the same scam, the one Dad got caught up in?"

"Then I'll find out, won't I?" Brook replied.

"And so will others. People will start asking questions, and *then* Dad's story will be interesting. *Then* our relationship with a number of governments, including our own, will be in jeopardy."

"I know the risk," Brook said, standing and getting ready to leave.

"Do you?" Carl challenged. "It's not just my livelihood. I've got a wife and those girls to look after."

"Oh, please," she sighed. "Don't put that on me. I'll be careful."

"What about the Middle East? What you've got hold of could light it up like a Roman candle."

Brook sat down hard with a laugh. "It's already lit; they don't need me to supply the matches. The Turks are fighting the Kurds, the Shiites are fighting the Sunis, and the Iranians are fighting Israel, who is fighting everybody. Throw in Russia and the Western powers, and I don't see how I could possibly make it worse. You give me too much credit."

With that, Brook stood again, the conversation over. If Carl were able to stop her from going, he would have said so by now.

"We won't support you. The foundation, I mean."

"I don't expect you to. I'm on sabbatical at half-pay and I've already lined up some backing. Being a superstar isn't all misery, you know. There's money in it."

"You're doing commercials for Burma Shave?" Carl smiled.

"Not exactly," Brook replied wryly. She wasn't angry with her brother, and Carl didn't seem angry with her anymore, not really.

9

Lev Abramovich was ready to beat the crap out of his friend, Natan, for dragging him into this tunnel. Natan was one for bright ideas...especially bright ideas that got Lev injured or in trouble. Lev should never have told Natan that he had found that old map in the mausoleum under the synagogue.

He had been helping to clean it out, removing old books and at least half a millennium's worth of junk. Sheer curiosity got the best of him, and he began leafing through a stack of books written in German—which he could read most of given his first language was Yiddish. A particularly tattered book caught his eye, completely falling apart when he picked it up. One page was much larger than the others, folded up, and appeared to contain plans for *Die Bibliothek des Zares von Moskau*—The Library of the Tsar of Moscow. It outlined the specifications and the proposed dimensions, and on the back was a map detailing the site of an entrance to one of the service tunnels leading from the Moscow

River. Lev knew the location.

To go into the tunnels of Moscow was extremely dangerous, he had heard. It wasn't only that the tunnels themselves—hundreds of years old—were capable of collapse at any moment, could flood, were filled with rats, or were incubators for all sorts of horrible diseases; the biggest danger was from Stalin's Red Guards, who patrolled the massive tunnel system under and around the Kremlin on a daily basis on the direct orders of the Secretary General himself, whose paranoia knew no bounds, and whose lust for killing was insatiable.

"They'll accuse us of plotting a *coup d'etat*," Lev complained as the two boys discussed the discovery the next day. "They'll shoot us on the spot."

"That's the genius of your map," Natan told him. "It shows an *unknown* tunnel. How are the guards going to patrol an *unknown* tunnel?"

Lev wasn't buying the logic, but he'd never been able to say "no" to Natan. Whatever happened, being his best friend was always an adventure, and Lev, a typical Russian teenager, loved adventure, though it was generally Lev, not Natan, who ended up paying for it later.

"See?" Natan nudged Lev, who was acting surly and put-upon, and seemed ready to refuse. "Anyway, we shouldn't run away from trouble; if we hadn't gotten into trouble, you would never have had to clean up the mausoleum, and we never would have found this map."

"*We* didn't get in trouble," Lev reminded Natan, "*I* got into trouble, because of you, and *I* found the map, not *you.*"

"That's true," Natan admitted. "All I'm saying is that this is destiny. This was meant to happen. It's our fate to discover something wonderful down there. All the signs point to it. Nothing can stop us, nothing can harm us."

That kind of talk was the sort of thing that made Lev desperately afraid of being anywhere near Natan, in case *HaShem* himself were to take the time to strike them both dead for such brazen *chutzpah*.

"I think I should show this to the rabbi," Lev said uneasily.

"No!" Natan protested. "That would be the exact wrong thing to do."

"It's just plans for a library—"

"The *Tsar's* library!"

"Which is why we could get killed."

"The Tsar's *lost* library," Natan replied. "Ivan the Terrible's *lost* library. It's disappeared. Nobody's seen it for five hundred years. Don't you know anything? It's one of the great mysteries of this cruel country; can you imagine the treasures, the valuable manuscripts, documents, and artifacts? We'll be rich, Lev, *rich!*"

* * *

There was just enough moonlight that night for Lev and Natan to see their way along the river bank, yet it was still dark enough that nobody could see them more than 20 yards away. The two teens had spent the afternoon copying the map by hand—the object itself was just too fragile to bring along on an outing like this.

"And besides," Natan had argued, "the map alone is probably worth a fortune."

Every ten minutes or so, the boys dared to light a match for a minute and studied their map, trying to gauge exactly where the tunnel began. It wasn't a simple feat; the river had changed over five centuries.

"Here," Natan insisted after they had walked for a while. "It has to be here."

"Where?" Lev asked, seeing only a bank of mud identical to all the other banks of mud they'd passed on the way to this spot. It had been a wet winter and a muddy spring.

"Under there," Natan decided, pointing for emphasis. "We need to dig."

"With what? We have no shovels," Lev whispered. Even though they were down on the riverbank, it was still situated in the heart of the city of Moscow, and a passer-by could easily hear them and alert the authorities.

"With our hands," Natan answered, dropping to his knees and beginning the process.

"This is the wrong place," Lev complained after they'd dug through a foot of wet silt.

"We just have to dig deeper," Natan replied insistently.

"It's a waste of time."

"If this is the wrong place, we'll just have to come back tomorrow night and try elsewhere."

"I have to work at the mausoleum during the day," Lev whined.

"I worked today, and I have to work tomorrow. When will I sleep?"

"You'll sleep when we're *rich!*" Natan exclaimed, his voice just above a whisper.

"I'll sleep when I—" Lev's words were cut off by the dull sound of his fist making contact with metal.

"…I'm dead," he finished, his voice trailing off.

The two boys looked at each other for a few seconds, and then attacked the digging with a new-found fervor, finally revealing the entirety of a large metal door. A rusty lock was easily broken, and the doors had been pried open wide enough for the two teens to slip inside.

"Now we need a lantern," Natan remarked, lighting a match and finding himself staring down a long corridor half-filled with silt.

"Look!" Lev hurried over to a wall lamp of sorts—a candleholder with a six-inch length of wax stuck in the brass. "Bring your match."

Careful not to let the match go out—they were down to half a dozen now—Natan lit the candle. "Somebody's been down here," he managed, voice quivering, suddenly not as brave as he once was once.

"It's an old candleholder," Lev pointed out, trying to calm his friend. "Maybe very old."

"But the candle is fresh!"

"How long do candles last? Forever, I think," Lev offered optimistically.

Still, it seemed like Natan was now getting cold feet. "What if the Bolsheviks find us? What if we get stuck down here?" he said in a panic.

"Shut up and follow me," Lev spat, annoyed at Natan's sudden cowardice after forcing him to come down here in the first place. He headed further down the tunnel without another word. Natan, not wanting to be alone in the dark, followed quickly despite his nervousness. In places, the tunnel was so constricted with silt that the boys had to crawl. Eventually, they made it to another door, this one seemingly guarded by two skeletons.

"Not guards," Lev observed, watching his friend's eyes widen and dart stealthily over his shoulder to check they were alone. "Look! They were crucified." He pointed out how the bones were pinned to the wall.

"I'm going to be sick," Natan moaned, swooning.

Lev grabbed him before he fell to the floor and slapped his face a couple of times. There was no need to say anything. This had been Natan's idea, but he wasn't man enough to carry it through. Lev pried the door open just enough to squeeze in. The candle threw enough light to allow him to make out an enormous chamber containing shelves upon shelves of books. They were also strewn across the floor, as odd shelves had collapsed over the centuries. Lev picked up one volume and wiped the thick muck off of the cover. He cracked it open.

"Greek," he guessed, showing Natan. The other boy looked desperately ill, and wasn't much interested. "Should we get out of here?" he asked calmly.

"Yes, please," Natan answered.

Though he was tempted to show no mercy, Lev could see that their candle was already half gone, and although the tunnel had been relatively straight, with no intersections or other paths, they couldn't be sure of that for the rest of the way, and neither boy wanted to be trapped in the dark.

"Just one more minute," Lev said, mostly to make Natan suffer a little longer. He opened one of the chests that were scattered everywhere and retrieved a book that appeared to be in decent shape and of a convenient size to fit in his pocket. "A sample," he muttered to himself.

They crawled back, reaching the river long before dawn, and used the rest of the cover of darkness to push the silt back over the doors and note the landmarks above the banks.

"If you don't want to come back here," Lev told Natan, "you don't have to. But don't tell anyone."

"I won't," Natan agreed, passing no comment about whether he'd return or not.

Lev shook his head. He'd never heard of the Lost Library, but they'd found it, and it was obvious the sheer quantity of material contained within it meant they'd be rich beyond their wildest dreams. And yet, faced with a couple of skeletons and a dark tunnel, Natan was letting his fear get the better of him.

"I have to get home to sleep," Lev said simply, though he knew that would be impossible now. "I have to work today."

10

Ammann, Jordan

Brook arrived in Amman, Jordan, after traveling for over twenty-four hours. She had taken the cheapest flight, with a dismal layover in Jeddah, Saudi Arabia, and had to cancel several more speaking engagements, as well as an interview with National Geographic. That last one had hurt. She'd offered to reschedule, and they had said they'd get back to her, but Brook took that to be code for, "You were hot for a minute there, but nobody's interested in you anymore."

Ouch, Brook told herself as she stepped off the plane. Now, with a bit of time to reflect on the outcome, she grinned to herself. She was quietly thrilled at the possibility of melting back into obscurity.

Waiting for Brook was Pejna Barzanji, a Kurdish-Syrian national who Brook had studied and done field work alongside since her first dig in the Middle East. They had stayed in touch on-and-off and on through the years, but as Pejna waved her over,

Brook hardly recognized her old friend. Pejna looked very different now, possessing a thicker, more muscular frame, and hollow sunken eyes.

Brook found herself shocked by Pejna's appearance. It had been seven years since she'd seen her friend, and those years had obviously been hard ones.

They embraced first, then Pejna reached out a mangled right hand, half of it missing, and unashamedly shook Brook's hand with a hard, heavy grip.

"Pejna," Brook breathed with a gasp, holding back tears.

"It is a long, sad story," Pejna said evenly. "I will tell it to you sometime."

They took a cab into the city, Pejna glancing out of the back every once in a while, unknowingly spiking Brook's paranoia

"Are you making sure we're being followed, or are you making sure we're *not* being followed?" she asked finally.

"I'm sorry. It's a habit. You know..." Pejna trailed off with a pointed look to the cabbie.

"You'll tell me later?" Brook whispered.

Pejna nodded.

When they reached Pejna's apartment, a tiny two-room place built over a candy store, she outlined the basics.

"I am a refugee," she said. "I have spent the last five years fighting both ISIS and the Syrian regime. But this..." she held up her hand, "is not my only injury. I was also hit in the head, and sustained brain damage. With the hand, I can still fight, but with the brain, I can no longer, so I am free to do the archaeology I was trained for."

"I...I don't know what to say," Brook said. "I'm sorry for your troubles."

"I suspect you haven't had it so easy yourself," Pejna ventured.

"I've had my battles," Brook told her friend, "but nothing like yours."

"Many have had it worse. With half a brain, I am still good for something," Pejna joked bitterly. "We will talk this evening. You should sleep now and acclimate yourself to local time. I will go to work and be back in approximately ten hours. No one will bother you here. There is no phone; do not answer the door. There is an extra key hanging just there, but maybe it would be better for you not to go out—the neighborhood is not very safe for a foreign woman alone."

"Thank you, Pejna."

"You are most welcome, my friend," Pejna said, before turning and hurrying out. Brook could hear the key in the lock, then Pejna's feet on the stairs.

.

11

Brook woke in the early evening. The sun was just going down, it was spring, and she could hear the streets of Amman come alive below as the people took advantage of the cool evenings and lengthening sunlight. Brook found the coffee pot and some coffee and made herself a few cups on the stove. As she sipped, she checked her phone, which was just the way she liked it; free of calls. Brook opened her laptop to see how many hundreds of e-mails she'd received, but balked at the thought of a sea of offers to "friend" her and inquiries from far and wide.

Brook shut the computer. She'd wait; there was no need to deal with that now. There might not even be an internet connection, let alone a router or whatever—technical details had always eluded her, and she was suddenly grateful for the University's IT Department and her automatic connections back in the States, as well as the more technologically minded members of the teams that usually accompanied her on the road. Resigning herself to staying offline, Brook picked up her coffee and made a tour of Pejna's meager digs.

There wasn't much to see; this was obviously a temporary home, judging by the few items of clothing that had been washed in the sink and hung up outside a window. There were also family photographs of unfamiliar faces. As close as Pejna and Brook had been, Brook had never known much the other woman's family, but now a particular photo caught her eye; showing Pejna with two small children she guessed to be three or four years old.

The sound of a key in the lock made Brook jump and spill a little coffee on her hand. She yelped, preparing to toss the coffee at the face of whoever was barging through the door.

"Oh, hi," Pejna said as she pushed it open. She was breathless, as if someone had been chasing her.

"Are you all right?" Brook asked, worried.

"Yes, I missed the bus and I didn't want to wait for another one and leave you here alone longer than I had to, so I walked. It's not far."

"I'm so sorry," Brook said. "I would have been fine."

"I know," Pejna replied. She sat down on the bed, leaving the one chair for Brook.

"Who are the children?" Brook asked, holding up the photograph.

Pejna paused, as if she weren't sure.

"That is Soran and Yelda," she said finally. "Soran is my son, aged four; Yelda is my daughter, aged three."

Brook was stunned, and had a hundred questions, but smiled, trying to be cheerful. "You never told me you had children!"

"Yes. They are the joy of my life," Pejna stated stoically, though her eyes shone with tears. She took the picture from Brook to look at it as if for the first time.

"Are you married?"

"I was married once," Pejna admitted.

"You never told me that!"

"He was killed."

"Oh, I'm sorry."

"He was not the father," she said matter-of-factly, putting the picture carefully back on the dresser. "I had many lovers after my husband died, though many of them were killed or wounded. This last lover is the father of Soran and Yelda. He wants to marry me, but I refuse. I fear if he marries me, he will die like the other."

Brook tried to smile sympathetically, still reeling from what she had just heard.

"Don't feel worry for them," Pejna said, suddenly jumping up and heading for the kitchen. "They knew what they were getting into. Shall I make supper?"

"I... sure..."

"You are hungry?"

"Yes, actually," Brook admitted. "But let me buy you dinner. We can go out."

"No, no," Pejna said. "I am too tired, and the places around here are all..." she trailed off with a grin. "The food is mysterious, let us say, and not in a good way."

Brook laughed.

Pejna lit the stove and put on a pot of boiling water before heating oil in a frying pan. It was all done with her one good hand, which amazed Brook.

"How about you?" Pejna asked. "When are you going to get married and have puppies?"

"Since you put it that way, never!" Brook laughed.

"Oh, surely there must be an assistant professor, a bright, young grad student, a Dean of Student Housing—"

"Not talking," Brook avowed.

"—or some rich ex-Wall Street type?" Pejna finished wryly.

"Okay," Brook sighed. "I guess I walked into that one."

"We get the gossip columns even over here," Pejna advised, "and you, Brook Burlington, are a celebrity whether you like it or not. Mr. Tom Manor is too."

"Guilty."

"So, it's true—you *are* an item!"

"Honestly, I don't know. We haven't sorted it out." Brook breathed in deeply, "God, that smells good—what are you cooking?"

"Just *tapsi*. Eggplant, zucchini, onion, and a little beef— leftovers, really. As soon as the rice is done, we'll eat."

"So the children, they're with their father?" Brook asked, eager to move the topic of conversation away from her relationship with Tom.

"For the time being."

"Do you have a picture of him?"

Pejna shook her head.

"Too dangerous," she said softly. "I don't even speak his name. For the time being, they are safe, that's all I know."

"Fair enough," Brook answered. It sounded lame, but she had no other words. 'Sorry for your troubles' wouldn't cut it, either.

"But the dig!" Pejna blurted, smiling brightly, "The dig is a good thing. There is a Bronze Age ruin right outside of Amman, just recently uncovered. It was destroyed and abandoned around 2100 BC."

"The Bronze Age Collapse?"

"Exactly," Pejna agreed.

"That's your specialty, isn't it? At least, it used to be."

"Right again," Pejna said. "It's a fascinating period, with so many parallels to our current situation. It's a time of climate change, war, and famine—so similar to what's happening in Syria, Iraq, and Lebanon today. What becomes of the Fertile Crescent when it's not so fertile? Collapse spreads, you know. It's a communicable disease, like a pandemic."

"It sounds incredibly interesting," Brook told her friend.

"I think so, but how about you? What project have you come all the way here to do, and how can I help you with it?"

"Can we eat first?" Brook laughed, stalling.

"Certainly."

The food was as delicious as it smelled. Brook had never taken Pejna for a cook; revolutionary, political firebrand, and a warrior for the cause of her people, yes; but not a cook.

"I love the digging," Pejna confided at the end of the meal, "but when I return home, I intend to become a politician. Run for office. I can do so much more to further archaeology that way, though that's not the main reason, of course. There is so much that needs exploring."

Brook nodded, agreeing, but wondered if she'd called the wrong person. She hated to lie to her old friend, or withhold information from her, but the fact was that she would be investigating the validity of a hundred-year-old agreement between the Kurds, the Arabs, and the Western Powers that Pejna would not like to discover her people had been cheated out of

"I can't tell you how unfair this has been," she continued bitterly. "We fought against Saddam, the Iraqis, the Persians, ISIS and all the other jihadists, against Assad, the Syrian regime, and even the Russians. All with the idea—the *understanding*—that we would get our own autonomous nation when it was over. Kurdistan is all we want. ,Nobody else wants that for us."

Yeah, it's happening all over again, Brook thought. *Your people are going to get the short end of the stick, my old friend, just as it happened before—vetoed by the Turks.*

"I envy you," she blurted after a pause.

Pejna laughed. "Are you joking with me? You have everything; I have nothing, not even a country."

"You have a cause you believe in."

"You have your work, which the whole world knows about. That is something."

"Archaeology matters?" Brook said cynically.

"Yes, it matters," Pejna insisted. "Now let's stop talking about unhappy things. I made yellow rose-petal dessert." She got up, went to the icebox, retrieved a pan, and put it on the stove. "Just for you. I just need to warm it up."

"I'm honored."

"It's a perfect dessert for us, for this moment. The rose petals are bitter and sour, but with enough boiling and sugar, that taste will be gone, and we will enjoy the sweetness of our lives."

"Amen," Brook smiled.

12

Moscow, 1926

"Do you know Avram, the bookseller on Chestnut Street?" Lev asked his uncle Theo as casually as he could.

"I do," Uncle Theo said. "Why do you ask?"

"I wonder what you think of him."

"And why is that? Are you thinking of marrying one of his daughters?"

"I didn't know he had daughters."

"Yes, two, I believe. Not that attractive. I would suggest you look elsewhere."

"Uncle Theo, I'm not getting married."

"Good for you, young man. Smart move. I approve!" Theo said with a twinkle in his eye. Lev understood his uncle was teasing him now, and he had no time for that. He had a book in his pocket—burning a hole in there, it felt like—written in either Greek or Latin. Lev couldn't tell which, but one thing he did know was that he had a strong need to discover its value.

"Avram, the bookseller...?" he asked again. "As a businessman, *not* a father," he added pointedly.

Theo considered the question, and Lev waited. He knew his uncle considered himself a bit of a scholar, or a rabbi of sorts, even if that wasn't acknowledged by anyone else.

"According to the mitzvah of *dan l'kaf zechut*," Uncle Theo intoned, raising one finger in the air in a gesture that threatened to deliver a sermon, "one must not judge another. One must give other people the benefit of the doubt, and not engage in idle gossip. Even the dust of *lashon hara* is forbidden."

Lev huffed, but continued to wait. He knew there was more.

"However," Theo said quietly, "since you are my beloved nephew, I will offer the advice that you should steer clear of Avram, understanding that certain idle slanderers and scandalmongers may have mentioned in the past that he is a despicable back-stabber, double-crosser, and deals in stolen goods on occasion." He tapped the side of his nose just to be sure Lev got the message.

"Thank you, uncle," Lev answered. It was the answer he had hoped for; he had no need for an honest man in this venture. An honest man might guess the source of the book, and take the matter right to the authorities.

*   *   *

"Nearly worthless," Avram the bookseller told Lev. "I'm not interested." He turned his back on the teenager and went about his business again.

"What about this one?" Lev asked, stowing the shabby, well-worn Gogol reprint away and replacing it with the volume from his pocket.

Avram took a quick look, visibly stopping himself from doing a double take. Lev too hid his excitement—it was impossible to miss the tiny gleam in the bookseller's eye.

"Again, not much here," Avram said, but his fingers were careful with this one as he skimmed the pages. "I'm thinking of a price..." he shrugged his shoulders dismissively.

You should be on the stage, Lev thought.

"Where did you get this, my young friend?" Avram asked casually.

"I found it," Lev replied.

"But where?"

"I don't remember."

"Might there be other books to be found where you forgot you found this one?" the bookseller pressed.

"Do you want to buy it or not?" Lev shot back.

"I want to give you a fair price," Avram lied, taking his hands from the book. Suddenly, it was like the thing was poison to his touch. "If you would leave it for me to study, I could ascertain its full value. Here," the bookseller fished out a coin and pushed it across the counter. "Take this for one night's reading. Come back tomorrow, and I will make you an offer. If you don't like it, keep the coin, and you will have an appraisal."

"I'm not a lending library," Lev protested, as tempting as the coin was. His family was poor, but his mother and father worked hard, and so did his siblings. He ached to be able to give them an easier life.

Shaking his head, he picked up the book again.

"Please, young man," Avram begged as Lev started for the door. "Don't you trust me?"

Lev stopped. Somehow, he felt this might be his one shot to sell the book and get his way.

"My religion teaches me to give every person the benefit of the doubt," he replied evenly.

"Ha!" the bookseller laughed, throwing up his arms, delighted by the answer. "Well said!" The man tapped his nose and pointed his finger at Lev as though sharing some private intimacy. "I like you. You come back with that book tomorrow and I will buy it...maybe for more than you might expect."

Lev didn't reply, and left quickly.

The streets of Moscow looked just the same as before, bustling with people in a hurry to make something of themselves; yet he found himself feeling more anxious and worried than ever.

"Dangerous," Lev muttered, fingering the object in his pocket. *This is all Natan's fault.*

*　　*　　*

They came in the middle of the night, waking the entire neighborhood—big, rough men in coarse clothing shouting orders to Lev's family members, pulling him out of bed.

"Where's the book?" they screamed.

"What book?"

SLAP, PUNCH. Lev's mother screamed, and they punched her, too, twisting her arm behind her back and shoving her in Lev's face. Desperate to protect her, Lev quickly retrieved the book from under his underwear in the dresser. They rushed him into a black car surrounded by other black cars, and drove the short trip to a bare-walled dungeon.

Valery Strelov, Special Section, Joint State Political Directorate (OGPU), was clearly not a man versed in rare books. He took a quick look at the words, which were written in an ancient language he could not decipher, and put it aside. Strelov was short but powerfully built, with steely eyes that were impossible to read. Though only a year or two older than Lev, Strelov's short life had been one long and vicious series of dog-fights, each of which Strelov had managed to win no matter what the odds were against him.

"Leave us alone," Strelov told the henchmen who'd brought Lev in, waving them away with a flick of his wrist.

Lev was chained to a steel table. He sat on a hard steel chair and was freezing, still in pajamas. He couldn't help but notice the dark stains everywhere—dried blood? *Probably.* He swallowed hard.

Strelov, on the other hand, looked entirely comfortable. He wore no uniform, only the gray suit of the oppressor.

"We won't discuss this book...yet." Strelov began, moving in closer. "What I am interested in is the *map.*"

Lev nodded. He knew there was no use arguing. Whatever Strelov chose to dish out, he wouldn't be able to take it. The young man slumped to the steel table and bawled his eyes out as if his life depended on it, and it did.

"Okay, that's enough," Strelov whispered softly after a minute or two, caressing Lev's curly hair. "Tell me."

Lev sat up slowly and told Strelov everything.

How Natan had found a map and used it to sneak around in the tunnels below the Kremlin.

How Natan had crawled around and found what he thought was a hidden library.

How Natan had had no idea what he'd come across.

How Lev had agreed to try and sell the book for Natan, in exchange for a cut of the profits both now and for the other books Natan might steal from the library.

"I have no idea how to find the tunnel," Lev concluded shakily. "It's on the map."

"Which is where?" Strelov asked.

"Natan has it," Lev told him.

"You've seen this map?"

Lev shook his head with a wry smile—a silent "are you kidding?"

"Natan is my best friend," Lev spoke aloud, "but he doesn't trust me."

Strelov snickered; and Lev joined him in appreciating the irony of the situation; a delicate bond forming between the two.

"He'll give it to you if you ask," Lev pleaded sincerely, man-to-man. "There's no need to hurt him."

"I understand—he is your friend."

"Don't tell him I told you."

Strelov shrugged.

"I don't see how it can be helped," the OGPU man told Lev, who started to cry again.

*   *   *

They dumped Lev on the sidewalk in front of his apartment building, tossing him out from a moving car. His mother and father were frantic, and it looked like the whole neighborhood had been roused. The nearby synagogue had been raided and ransacked, the rabbi detained, and every inch of Lev's apartment searched.

"There isn't much time," Lev told his mother, pushing her away when she tried to clean his cuts and put pressure on his bruises. He was already packing a bag.

"Where are you going?" Lev's father demanded.

"It's better you don't know," Lev replied simply.

13

"So we're going to Petra?" Pejna asked the next day.

"*I'm* going to Petra," Brook answered. "I appreciate you setting this up, but you have a job."

"Which I will still have," Pejna replied. "They're giving me leave for a few days on full pay. They're thrilled to death, actually—a connection with you, no matter how tenuous, is a valuable one."

Brook raised an eyebrow cynically. "I don't believe it."

"You're famous, you know."

"I've heard that," Brook replied sarcastically. "You didn't tell them I was coming, did you?" she added, suddenly alarmed.

"No! You told me not to; I wouldn't. But they knew, and they knew I was associated with you. I don't know how."

* * *

Brook's father had had his failings, but for all his faults Cale Burlington had undeniably been an exceptional archaeologist. From her father's notations, she had easily located the exact spot where he claimed to have found T.E. Lawrence's belongings.

Brook looked around. This was Petra, one of the most famous sites in the world, and once the capital of a great ancient empire. It was the crossroads of Asia, Europe, Egypt, and Africa, made famous by the Indiana Jones movies. She was still capable of being stunned by its oversized beauty, and the ornateness of its carvings—its tombs, its temples, and its *history!*

"This is where my father's professional life came to an abrupt, crushing halt," Brook told Pejna.

They stared into a vast chasm—a dig site ten feet deep and set away from the magnificent architectural formations. Here, in this completely unremarkable side-alley, lay a remarkable history. It was here that Lawrence and his Arab warriors had hidden from the Ottomans, darting out to wage bloody battle, then retreating. The contrast was striking—ancient magnificence turned back to cave dwelling; riches into carnage. Civilization had become rubble.

"The 20th-century..." Brook cursed under her breath.

"Excuse me?" Pejna asked.

"If there was anything left of Lawrence here after the war, it's long gone now," Brook replied.

"You're right about that!" called a voice from nearby.

It was Saleh Ahmad, an old friend and co-worker of Cale's. He was older, but Brook recognized him right away; his grinning exuberance and lust for life hadn't aged a day.

"Mister Ahmad!" Brook almost screamed, running over to shake his hand vigorously.

"Call me Saleh, please, Miss Brook."

"It's been so long."

"You were just a little girl the last time I saw you," Saleh told her, smiling.

They looked each other over. Brook couldn't keep the tears from flowing down her cheeks, and blubbered an introduction to Pejna. She and Saleh shook hands, murmuring greetings in Arabic.

"This is the last place I saw your father," Saleh told Brook. "It wasn't a happy time, I must say." He shrugged dismissively. Unlike her father, it was clear that the setback had not broken the man's spirit. "We found many things that belonged to the Arab resistance, and to Mr. Lawrence, but it's all moved on now, I'm afraid. I've talked to the locals. Even the thieves don't come here anymore, but all is not lost. I believe I know who those thieves are, and I have an idea who their buyer would be."

"Let's go talk to them," Brook said.

Saleh shook his head. "No one will talk to you, but they might talk to me. And if there's money to be paid for information—well, you're a famous American archaeologist..."

"Who isn't rich," Brook finished pointedly.

"They don't know that," Saleh reminded her, looking to Pejna, who nodded a confirmation. "The best thing is for you two to be patient and wait in the hotel. I will see who I still know around here, and what they're willing to tell me."

*   *   *

When they met for dinner later that evening, Saleh proclaimed his inquiries a major success.

"You should go to Amman tomorrow," he announced. "I

believe I know where you should look, but again, I must accompany you."

"Okay," Brook agreed. "We'll all go."

"Now, I propose a toast to your father," Saleh said, lifting his glass of tea. "The greatest archaeologist of all time."

"Don't get carried away," Brook blushed, though she raised her tea as well.

"Well he was a great *guy*, " Saleh said, "no matter what happened to him professionally. *That* you can't take away; he was a genuine, decent human being."

Brook nodded, feeling pleased, and for the first time in a while, comfortable.

Saleh spoke on through supper, recounting adventures had between himself and her father. Brook tried to listen attentively, but her mind also wandered—she'd heard most of those tall tales before. Through it all, Saleh—a gentleman—didn't mention the end, not that she knew much of it herself. In his last days, Cale hadn't shared much about the particulars of his downward spiral. Brook knew he was embarrassed, and had always guessed he didn't want to impose his suffering on his family.

Pejna, however, listened closely. She learnt that Cale had been convinced of the "missing links" between ancient civilizations in the Middle East, South America, Southeast Asia, Polynesia and South America. As a result, Cale was ripe for the ruse concocted by hedge-fund genius Raymond Manor—Tom's father, she remembered reading in one of the many gossip columns about him and Brook—and a Russian organized crime figure, Strelov, to use

Cale's considerable reputation to fund massive archaeological digs all over the world. For securing his friend's participation with a combination of his trust and this all-too-tempting lie, Jacob Linsky was rewarded with passes for his family to exit the dying Soviet Union.

"Do you remember Linsky?" Brook asked Saleh suddenly, interrupting his monologue.

"Oh yes," Saleh answered, chuckling a little. "I used to call him Santa Claus."

Brook smiled. That was the way she remembered him, too.

"I used to drive him around," Saleh went on. "I would drive him to the dig site, to the hotel, to eat, to meetings; lots of meetings. It kind of made me angry. I was a hot-shot archaeologist, I thought, but I was being treated like a secretary—"

"Meetings with who?" Brook blurted.

"Pfft! This I don't know. People who were important maybe, with money. And there were phone calls; I always had to take him to places that had phones—booths, restaurants, even stores. He would ask to use a phone and pay for the calls—always long distance. This was before mobile phones."

"Who was he calling?" Brook pressed, curious.

"Mostly one person," Saleh answered. "All over the world, now that I remember. In Moscow, Alexandria, Cairo. I thought it was unusual at the time. Once, I drove him to Amman, and I believe he met the man on the other end of the phone there. Maybe it was his boss; he was always sort of bowing and apologizing with his voice."

"Who was he?"

"I don't know," Saleh said, shaking his head. "I never heard a name. He sounded Russian, maybe. Big accent."

"What did he look like?"

Saleh laughed. "He looked like a criminal who had spent a lot of time in prison lifting weights," he said, miming the exercise. "Strong, but small. Short, I mean."

Brook sat back in her chair, trying to think. It could be a lot of people, she supposed.

Or it could be Strelov.

14

Jordan, Between Petra and Ammann

Pejna drove while Brook tried to rest on the way back to Amman. Saleh took up the rear in his own car.

"I hope you don't mind, but I got us all rooms at a hotel in Amman," she had told Saleh before they set off. "I thought it would be easier if the three of us stuck together."

"That makes sense," Saleh said. "I don't mind staying in a nice hotel with hot water and a soft bed."

"I thought you might agree to it," Brook smiled.

As they drove, her phone rang.

"Hello?"

"It's done!" Katy James announced proudly. Katy was Brook's best friend back from their days in undergrad.

"What's done?" Brook asked, just to bug her.

"The film, stupid, the film!"

Katy had documented the entire discovery of Cleopatra and Antony's resting place with her little camera, and had spent the last year editing the considerable footage and supplementing it with interviews and archival material. "I'm giving it the whole Ken Burns treatment!" she'd proclaimed.

"Well, congratulations," Brook said. "I'd like to see it sometime." she added, which wasn't true.

"You need to send me your schedule."

"What for?"

"You have to be there for the screenings, the premiere, and film festival season. The Cairo Film Festival is at the end of the year, but I don't want to wait that long. There's Academy Awards to think about, too—"

"Katy," Brook interrupted sharply, suddenly annoyed. She had become used to the world shoving her under the spotlight, but her best friend? "Leave me out of it. Thank you."

Before Katy could reply, she hung up her phone, put it on mute, and threw it in the glove compartment.

Pejna shot her a worried glance, but didn't say a word.

* * *

"May I get your bags, ma'am?" a familiar voice called from behind Brook as she stepped out of the car at the Amman hotel.

Brook turned and squealed, making the grinning Tom Manor start.

Brook jumped into his arms. As if driven by an invisible force, she pressed her lips to his. It was just what Brook needed at that moment; she would worry about the consequences later.

"How did you find me?" she asked when she'd caught her breath.

"I have my ways," he answered with a sly grin.

"Your ways!" Brook slugged him in the arm, only half angry. "Pejna, this fool is Tom Manor. Tom, this is my friend Pejna."

Tom and Pejna exchanged a smile confirming they were in on a secret that Brook was too giddy to decipher. After they had shaken hands, Tom picked up Brook's bag along with his own backpack, and they headed into the hotel.

"Did you check in?" Brook asked.

"No, not yet."

Brook grinned wryly. "Don't bother. I have a room." She spun on her heel to face Pejna and announced, "Just give them my name at the desk. See you tomorrow, okay?"

Pejna nodded with a knowing smile and watched as Brook and Tom went upstairs together.

* * *

In a passionate blur, she and Tom made love, ordered room service and ate supper, made love again, and fell asleep in each other's arms, waking in the wee hours of the morning.

"We are *definitely* going to need to talk about this later," Brook sighed as she snuggled against Tom's chest.

"Don't," Tom murmured back, theatrically pressing a finger to her lips.

"I still don't see how you knew I was here," Brook protested, swatting his hand away.

"I had some help."

"My brother told you."

"No, your brother was decidedly unhelpful," he complained. "I was contacted by a certain ex-resistance fighter who told me that her dear friend Brook was desperately in need of a visitor."

He grinned, and Brook sat up and scoffed, making a mental note to have words with Pejna later.

"You don't mind, do you? That I came to see you?"

"I mind that the world knows where I am and what I'm doing every second of the day," she huffed.

"That's not true, Brook, it really isn't. I hate to tell you this, but most people don't care about you."

Brook laughed. "You're such a..." she started to say, but couldn't find the word. "White bread", "prude", and "innocent" all occurred to her.

"Yeah, I know," Tom confessed, even without the accusation. "I am." He moved next to her, and she let him hold her again.

"So..." Brook asked, "did you put your jar in the overhead rack?"

Tom laughed. "No, actually, I bought a seat for it."

"Did you get the bereavement fare?" she said casually.

Tom gasped.

"You didn't!" he exclaimed, delighted at the idea.

"Yes, I did."

"Damn! I never thought of that."

"The ticket lady suggested it for the jar. It wasn't my idea—"

"Wait, wait, the *jar* got the lower fare?" Tom wanted to know.

"Yeah."

"*You're* the bereaved! The jar wasn't bereaved one bit."

Brook laughed. "We should have *both* gotten the lower fare, huh?"

"I should say so..." Tom agreed, shaking his head in mock disgust at the horrible injustice of it all.

Brook laughed again, and then sobered quickly—back to business.

"You want to know the real reason I don't want the world to know where I am and what I'm up to?" she asked.

Tom raised an eyebrow. "Paranoid schizophrenia?"

"No, actually," Brook answered seriously—mental illness wasn't something she was prepared to joke about just yet. "I need a little space to investigate something my dad dredged up before the world grabs it and uses it for its own purposes."

"That sounds reasonable," he replied thoughtfully. "What can I do to help?"

Brook gave his arm a grateful squeeze. "You always say the right thing."

"I know."

"I'm looking for artifacts—a document, actually-—my father might have dug up in Petra that later made its way to the Soviet Union."

"Which is where I come in," Tom realized. "You need me to pull strings, see what I can find, and do a little searching on the down low?"

"Bingo."

"Are you going to tell me what I'm looking for," Tom joked, "or am I just putting out a search for anything old and dusty?"

"I'll tell you," Brook said hesitantly, wondering if she was about to make a huge mistake. "It belonged to Lawrence of Arabia."

"Lawrence of Arabia?"

"Yes," Brook answered.

"Oh, so his old clothes, a hat, pair of riding boots—"

"I mentioned it was a document," Brook interrupted.

Is Tom serious enough about this, is he going to be the reliable partner I need?

She hated the fact she didn't trust her own judgment anymore.

"A document," she continued quickly, pushing aside her fear, "granting the Kurds statehood. Guaranteeing Kurdistan. It's quite possibly signed by France, Italy, the US, and the King of England."

Tom whistled.

"Maybe the Turks, too," Brook added.

Tom sucked in air, then let it out again sharply.

"That would be something, wouldn't it?" he said.

* * *

The next morning, in the lobby of the hotel, Saleh described the promising avenue of inquiry he had discovered.

"It's a shop in the Old City," he told Brook, Tom, and Pejna. "A bookshop—al-Nasrani's Books. He says he has what you're looking for, but only for you alone." Saleh gestured toward Brook. Tom pulled her aside.

"You can't go alone," he whispered intensely.

Brook dragged him even farther away from the others for a heated discussion that she soon won, asserting that there was nothing Tom or anyone else could do to stop her. Not even Tom's downcast expression could shake her conviction. After assuring them all she'd be okay, Brook took a cab into the Old City to venture out on her own through the narrow streets.

* * *

Despite Saleh's precise directions, Brook was soon lost in a labyrinth of alleyways and crowded streets. The music and the smells—from food and tobacco to incense and perfumes—reminded her that Amman was one of the oldest continuously inhabited cities on the planet. Another day, perhaps, she could savor it, but today she was on a mission.

She found what she was looking for down at the dead end of a dark, gloomy alley—a medieval-looking sign hanging outside a small shop that read: 'al-Nasrani's Books, est. 1810'.

Brook took a deep breath to drum up her courage, and walked in.

The mess was overwhelming. Books were stacked floor to ceiling in no particular order, and a thick, musty stench assaulted her nose, erasing the pleasant odors she'd just enjoyed outside. There seemed to be no one there, though with so many mountains of various volumes, it was impossible to tell even how many customers—let alone potential assassins—could be hiding in the small space.

Brook ventured further inside, and a pattern began to emerge from the madness. There appeared to be unlabeled sections for various religious books—including the Qur'an, Bible, and Talmud —and commentaries on them; some looked centuries old. There were books of seemingly every language, ranging in binding from new paperbacks to vellum-bound and illuminated manuscripts. She was astonished.

It's a museum! Brook realized.

The shopkeeper was an ancient, bearded man, bent at the waist, who greeted Brook enthusiastically.

"Ceud mìle fàilte!" he called.

Brook stared, having no idea what he was talking about.

Puzzled, the man tried again. "Χαίρετε! Sveiki!"

"English?" Brook asked warily.

"You are not English!" he gasped theatrically.

"American," Brook answered, amused by his reaction.

The man gasped again.

"I thought Scots Gaelic, Greek, or Latvian," he said smoothly. "Your red hair confused me."

"Sorry about that."

"Nonsense! Let me show you around the shop," the man said, guiding Brook to the far corners of his domain and suggesting titles, giving the dates of when the books arrived and running an entertaining monologue throughout.

His English wasn't half bad; Brook wondered if he could maintain this fluency in other languages as well.

"I expect haggling, of course, though as an American, I know you probably aren't much good at it," the man smiled. "It's because you abhor the practice, believing it's beneath you. For us, it's sport, a social game. We talk, we play, we argue—it's fun for us. But we can talk of other things first. You, for instance; are you married?"

Brook blushed.

"See?" the man said gleefully. "Even talk of your husband embarrasses you!"

"I'm not married," Brook answered with a smile, proving him wrong.

"Interesting! What do you do for a living?" he asked.

"I'm an archaeologist," Brook told him.

"Ah," the man said, pausing momentarily. Brook could see that this was the magic word he had been waiting for. "Come, come."

Glancing exaggeratedly over his shoulder, he led her to a different part of the shop. "There have been a few of you archaeologists in here over the years." The old man went straight to a book on one of the shelves and pulled it out carefully. It was a small volume that could easily fit into a pocket, wrapped in a canvas cover. "I found this just lying around the other day. I have no sense of my own inventory!"

The shopkeeper laughed and handed Brook the book. She took it out of its cover and opened it carefully.

"I think you might be one of very few people who will understand the importance of this book," the merchant told her. "One of very few."

Brook could see the book was very old, and written in Cyrillic script——now she wished Tom had come with her.

"A Polish Jew brought this book here many, many years ago— or was he Russian? It doesn't matter—Russian, Polish, all the same. He came through in the 1940s; I was just a boy then, but I remember him. He was on his way to the Holy Land, which was the first I'd heard of it. My father and grandfather were here then, and my uncle. He wore his shoes over his shoulders...they had holes in them, so he went barefoot. He must have walked a very long way, don't you think?"

Brook nodded, unsure what to make of the book or the story.

Was this why I was sent here? What's the old man trying to tell me anyway?

She closed the book and tried to hand it back, but the shopkeeper pushed it back to her. As he continued, it became apparent that there was nothing to do but let the man finish his tale.

"He brought this book. He said it was very valuable, and that he had found it in Moscow in a tunnel! Would you fancy that? He claimed it was Tsar Ivan the Terrible's book, part of a large collection.

"It is an interesting story," Brook replied, not sure what the man was trying to tell her. He seemed friendly enough, jovial even, and didn't appear that strong, even for his age. If he was trying to scare or threaten her, it wasn't working.

"The man who sold the book to my father to buy himself a meal and a decent pair of shoes said it had brought him nothing but misery. He said Stalin's guard had arrested his father, fascists had murdered his whole family, and he had taken nearly every wrong turn on his way to the Holy Land, which was how he ended up in Amman and not Jerusalem, where the other Jews were gathering to form Palestine. He said the book had been a weight around his neck, but I could see he was lying. The way he held it— how he would not let it leave his hands even though he was selling it—told me that it had kept him alive somehow through the horrors of life and war."

Brook understood that the book was very important to the old shopkeeper, too, a remnant of his youth.

"You want to buy the book?" the man asked, cutting the conversation short; before he could get sentimental, if Brook was correct.

"If you think I should," Brook answered. *"You and Saleh arranged this, correct?"* she wanted to ask, *"There's a clue buried in here that connects to my father and T.E. Lawrence somehow?"*

The shopkeeper gave her a wink, either confirming Brook's suspicion or simply flirting with the attractive American woman who had come through his door.

"I think you should have it," the man said simply.

"How much?" Brook asked.

He gave a price ten times what an ordinary artifact like this might cost, and Brook considered haggling.

"No, no," the shopkeeper chided, shaking a finger before she could open her mouth. "No haggling. You'll just embarrass yourself. I already respect your American way and give you my lowest price."

"Okay," Brook said. If she was being scammed, she didn't care. The man told a great story; he deserved what he could get.

15

Moscow, 1926

Valery Strelov wasn't worried when his dinner date was late. He knew Ignatius Stelletskii would show up sooner or later. Strelov was having the man followed, three teams of two men each working eight hour shifts twenty-four hours a day. Stelletskii knew it, too, and wouldn't dare try to slip out of the noose.

Despite the chill of early spring setting in, Strelov sat outside in a sidewalk cafe on Tverskaya Street, Moscow's most glamorous boulevard for the last six hundred years, though new buildings were being constructed at an alarming rate, and making noise. They were modern buildings, plain, proletarian, imposing, and brutal, so unlike the ornately decorated structures that already lined the street from years past.

The new architecture was an acquired taste, Strelov had decided, and he had yet to acquire it. Regardless, he would never say such a thing out loud; the Party forbade it. Yes; as tough a guy as Strelov was, he liked his buildings the way he liked his women—

soft, decorative, and decidedly impractical.

"Ah, there you are!" he called to Stelletskii as he advanced down the street. A half-block beyond the other man, Strelov watched his two employees pause and lean against a building as casually as they could, discussing the weather.

Stelletskii signaled to the waiter inside and took a seat across from Strelov, never hiding his disdain for the Special Section agent. Stelletskii, the older man of the two, was by then a famous Russian archaeologist; recognized worldwide, well educated, and one of the elite in a supposed society of equals.

"*Ukha*, salad, coffee," Stelletskii ordered briskly when he arrived.

Strelov had already eaten, evidenced by the empty soup-bowl and plate in front of him, but Stelletskii made no apology. In any other century, he and Strelov would never have occupied the same space, let alone spoken to each other. Even here, Stelletskii kept his wide-brimmed hat low over his eyes and pointed his face away from street, lest a friend, colleague, or old college chum spot him sitting there with the common thug they both knew Strelov to be, despite his powerful position within Soviet security apparatus.

"You said you had something for me," Stelletskii began without fanfare.

"I did have something for you, but I don't anymore," Strelov answered.

Stelletskii's face fell—the answer was not what he'd hoped.

"A book?" he croaked in disappointment.

"A small volume in Greek—very old. I retrieved it from a Jewish boy. He said he found it in a tunnel."

Stelletskii's brows rose, and his jaw widened. His gloved hands came out of his pockets and rested on the table palm-up, hoping to receive the precious book.

"Give it to me," he hissed urgently.

"I don't have it. I gave it back to the boy."

"You what?" Stelletskii asked, incredulous.

"I didn't know what it was at the time," Strelov admitted. He knew he'd made a mistake, but it was a misstep he vowed to never make again. Not once more would he trust a single soul during what he hoped would be long years of service to Mother Russia, no matter how many enemies it earned him. Every jaw broken or bullet fired was a brick in the foundation of the Soviet Utopia; a world he wanted his son to inhabit, worth all the blood and sacrifice.

Strelov had believed the kid—an enormous lapse in his judgment. As skilled a reader of the human condition as he had become, he'd made a mistake when it came to Lev Abramovich, who had reminded Strelov of the teenager he himself had been just a few years before.

Stelletskii was livid. If his food had arrived at that moment, Strelov was sure the famed archeologist—who'd spent his career searching for the Lost Library of Ivan the Terrible—would have thrown it in his face.

"Proof, damn you, proof!" Stelletskii screamed, his mind shooting ahead in the argument to someplace Strelov didn't understand.

"Proof?"

"The map! What happened to the map?! Did he have a map!? I heard there was a map!" Stelletskii screamed, no longer concerned with his position in society vis-a-vis the Special Section man.

The waiter, emerging from the cafe with Stelletskii's food, wisely hesitated.

"I destroyed it, lest it fall into the hands of traitors," Strelov stated simply.

He tensed for the volcanic eruption he was sure would follow. Strelov was young, strong, and versed in the more exotic arts of self-defense as well as straightforward and brutal wrestling and boxing moves—the elder Stelletskii wouldn't be a challenge.

In recognition of that fact, Stelletskii surrendered into himself; shrinking like the fog on a hot day, sitting back in his chair, and signaling for the waiter to serve the food. Hands shaking, the archaeologist ate like a starving man, as if the food would stave off the heart attack that was so obviously imminent. Finally, he put his fork and spoon down, drank his coffee, and spoke, never looking Strelov in the eye.

"Damn ideological idiots. Your minds are like dogs' minds, tugged around on leashes," he said.

Strelov said nothing.

"It'll be the ruin of us all."

Strelov shrugged slightly, not wanting to set the man off again. "Where is this Jewish boy with the book who found a tunnel?"

"Fled to Poland, we believe," Strelov replied.

"You gave him his book back, burned his map, and *let him emigrate?*" Stelletskii asked, incredulous.

Strelov gave a nod that indicated there was more to it than that, a silent reminder that the Special Section "had its ways" though Strelov himself knew it was a three-ring circus of a screw-up, and on his watch. "No more exceptions" was the best apology he could give.

Despite that, Strelov wasn't worried; Stelletskii wasn't his superior, and what was more, if he played the board correctly, Stelletskii would never *go* to Strelov's superiors. The damage to Strelov's career would be contained.

"There was another boy, too," Strelov said finally. "We dealt with him. He was just a snooping Jew."

"Dealt with him?"

"He won't be talking about the tunnels to anyone."

"Did you see the tunnels? Do you know where they are?" Stelletskii asked, suddenly excited.

"I know where the entrance to one is. I haven't gone inside, I want you with me when I do."

"Well, I'm here," Stelletskii answered, wiping his mustache and beard with his napkin, prepared to go charging blindly into whatever hole in the ground Strelov pointed him to.

"Not now," Strelov chuckled. "It's too dark and dangerous."

"Ah, and you don't want Lenin and Trotsky along for the ride," Stelletskii winked, jerking a thumb back at the two operators still waiting down the sidewalk.

"You guessed it, comrade," Strelov smiled. Now that Stelletskii was close to having everything he wanted in life, it didn't seem like having a Special Section agent for a friend was such a bad thing all of a sudden, he noticed. "I'll call the boys off and we'll meet here, say, tomorrow for breakfast? Seven a.m.?"

"I'll be here," Stelletskii assured the other man.

"Go on, now. I'll pay," Strelov told the archaeologist. "Tomorrow."

Stelletskii scurried off, deigning not to offer a thank you or give any kind of speech, though he'd felt one coming. He owed Strelov a huge debt of gratitude, one that he knew he'd certainly have to pay...

*   *   *

Valery Strelov recognized the cadence of the pounding on his door; he'd used that same rhythm himself a few times. It had to be the authorities wanting in, hitting the door hard enough to wake the entire building without bringing it down—without cooperation, that would come later.

Strelov jumped out of bed quickly and put on his shoes, calculating just how much time he had to leap from the fourth floor window. It was high, but it wasn't certain death, and anything else would be useless. He threw on pants and a shirt over his pajamas, ordering his wife to stay in bed and running to the other room where his daughter and beloved son slept, then ordering them to his wife's bedroom.

"Lock the door!" he shouted, hurrying to the front door, getting it open quickly, and throwing his hands up, taking the full brunt of the police's savage violence as it broke over him like a wave, knocking him to the floor. "Don't hurt them! Don't hurt my family! It's me you want, not them!"

There was blackness after that, and Strelov didn't see his family for months, or even know what had happened to them all through his trial and sentencing. He did not know his accusers, nor what he stood accused of beyond vague charges of 'treason' and 'crimes against the revolution'. Despite his 'confession', Strelov was still subjected to pain he never could have imagined would be possible. Because his record was blemish-free, his life was spared, and he was sentenced to hard labor in a Siberian gulag, where he was blessed to see his wife and children on rare occasions, waving from a nearby hill through the razor-wire fencing. His wife's infrequent letters explained that they had found him and taken up residence in a town nearby, a miserable, dilapidated settlement that had yet to be named by the local officialdom.

Sadly, he never got to reside there with them, as it was in the labor camp that Valery Strelov died a few years later from typhus.

16

Ocean City, MD / Amman, Jordan

"Hello?"

Retired Professor Stuart Green spoke into his flip-phone, a recent purchase. He walked the Ocean City boardwalk in Maryland with his dark brown Labrador Retriever named Memphis, another new acquisition. Since retiring from WVU, he'd been trying all sorts of new things; "baby steps into self-improvement", as he called them. He'd rented a large second-story apartment on St. Louis Avenue in the laid-back tourist Mecca, and could be seen every day on his walks, talking with real live people and giving little thought to the dead ones of his past. Gone were the sarcophagi, burial shrouds, and ancient embalming smells of his previous profession. His pale British skin refused to darken, however, and a shock of unkempt, snow-white hair still stuck out from under his Irish tweed hat.

"Professor Green?" Brook asked from the hotel lobby in Amman.

"Professor Burlington!" Green answered enthusiastically. "So good to hear from you."

The old professor's British accent was still there, Brook noted, but he sounded younger somehow.

"It's good to talk to you, too," Brook answered. "Is it a good time?"

"Perfect," the old archaeologist answered proudly. "I'm just walking Memphis on the boardwalk and speaking to you on my cell-phone."

"My, my," Brook replied, "isn't that progress?"

"Thank you for noticing," Green chuckled.

"I'm in Amman, Jordan, and I wondered if you might help me with something."

"If I'm able to, certainly."

"I'm interested in The Lost Library of the Tsars."

"Ah," Green replied, "the Golden Library."

"That's right," Brook confirmed.

"What's that got to do with Amman?" Green inquired.

"That's what I'm trying to figure out. I have a book that I bought here..."

Professor Green laughed, and took a seat on a bench in a quiet section of the walkway overlooking the Atlantic. "Let me guess," he said. "Some white-haired old man in a back-alley sold you a tea-stained book he claimed once resided in the Lost Library of the Tsars."

"Something like that," Brook replied, turning a little red. Now that she thought about it, it *did* sound preposterous.

"It's in Latin, I suppose," Green went on, ever the skeptic.

"Greek."

"Well, at least somebody did a *little* homework."

"The book looks authentic," Brook told Green, her voice sounding sharper than she'd intended. Yes, he sounded younger, and yes they had become closer in the last year, but Brook was quickly remembering how crusty he could be.

"You want to send it to me?" Green asked. "A few of us Faculty Emeritus types get together every other month or so. I could take it along, show a few of the Chitwood Hall chaps; the Russian History crowd."

"No, I wouldn't want to put it in the mail if it's what I think it might be."

"I understand," Green replied, but Brook could tell he was just humoring her.

"I was thinking more of scanning a few pages and emailing them over with the front and back covers."

"Worth trying," Green said. "You have my email; I'll see if any of my friends can figure it out."

"Thank you, Professor. You're very kind."

Green blustered a little—he wasn't used to compliments. Over the past couple of years, Green had come to think of Brook as a daughter, and it still meant a lot to him when she spoke to him, cared for his advice, or asked for his help. Green muttered his goodbyes quickly, careful not to say too much and embarrass himself.

Brook hung up the phone and immediately emailed him the pages from the book she'd already scanned, along with photos of the front and back cover and the binding on the side. As an afterthought, she also sent the pages and pictures to Tom Manor, who had left that morning for Moscow in pursuit of the Lawrence of Arabia document.

She had been reluctant to let him go so soon, but he had been certain. "The people I need to talk to do better business face to face over dinner and vodka. Lots and lots of vodka," he had explained.

Brook smiled, put her phone away and headed for the exit, every inch the woman on a mission.

Pejna, too, had recently abandoned Brook with a text message: "Returning to my Bronze Age ruin job. So good to see you again, call me."

Brook felt a little guilty about her old friend. The very hardship Pejna had faced had conspired to pull them apart. It wasn't Pejna's fault, but unbeknownst to her, the combination of her allegiances and the knowledge Brook possessed made their friendship dangerous. Brook sincerely vowed to do something about it when she could, and promised herself she would ensure she and Pejna would be fast friends again; they just had to be.

As many times as she had visited Amman, its streets and thoroughfares always awed Brook. As she walked down the street, she noted how the people moved in complicated ways, no two going in exactly the same direction, moving like a woven rug of humanity. Sellers called out to the tourists, but unlike other places in the Middle East, they wouldn't think of dragging you into a tiny shop or kiosk—these city merchants were too sophisticated for that sort of thing. They never had to push for a sale; the sheer quantity of pedestrians passing through ensured an ever-ready stream of customers. The *souqs,* open-air markets, sold everything from fruits and vegetables to fish and lamb, and the street-food aromas were almost overwhelming.

Booksellers were everywhere, spreading their wares directly on the sidewalk or blankets. Brook was suddenly all too aware of the priceless volume in her purse, and held it tighter to her side under her long jacket. The odds of finding something similar from one of these street-vendors were astronomical, but she was a digger both by trade and inclination, so who knew where the next find would come from? She was surprised to see a number of contemporary popular novels, some with racy titles, among the offerings. The government censors were no doubt spending more time on news reports, websites, and emails these days than the fading publishing industry.

Besides her general browsing of the books on offer, Brook had one specific volume in mind, and had already located where it was available. She stood outside the window of a high-end shop catering to the rich elite and foreign tourists with Western reading habits, and quickly spotted it; *Finding Cleopatra* by Thomas H. Manor. Brook stared at the display with mixed emotions. There were 50 copies there, she guessed, carefully arranged. To her surprise, a tower of books stood alongside them, these in Arabic. Tom hadn't told her there was a translation! In fact, Tom hadn't said anything at all about the book—to protect Brook's feelings, no doubt.

Part of him had been right, she realised as she fought back the pang of jealousy that had developed the moment she has first spotted the books. By rights, it should have been Brook's book sitting there in the window, but he'd had the vision, time, determination, and mental stability to write it, and she hadn't.

Brook choked, swallowing tears. She had tried to be grown up about it, and had even read the book in draft form as Tom had requested.

"I don't want to drive in your lane, rain on your parade, steal your thunder or anything like that," he had explained when he asked to send it to her. "On the other hand, if I got anything wrong or offended you in any way, I want to know about it before it goes to the printers. If you want me to tear the thing up, I'll do it, just let me know. I won't burn it though, smog being what it is with global warming and all."

She'd swallowed her feelings and had read the book. It was a personal story of Tom's journey— more of a memoir, really—and besides the fact he had scrupulously avoided much of the archeological details to avoid encroaching on Brook's territory, she found no fault with it besides a few details she was able to correct.

"My biggest issue is grammar," she told him once she had finished. "Your grammar's terrible!"

"The publisher has people for that," Tom had grinned, incredibly relieved at her reaction.

That had happened months ago, and now, here it was. Tearing

her eyes away from the window, Brook went into the shop and bought four copies; two English, two Arabic. If the clerk thought this was unusual, he didn't say anything. She would have bought more; to give to Pejna maybe, and Saleh, but their weight was about all she could carry on foot—she'd walked a long way from the hotel, and still had a long way to go.

As she continued on her journey, Brook had the distinct sense she was being followed, and tried to ignore it— it was something she'd discussed at length with her therapist after her breakdown.

The streets are teeming with people, Brook told herself. *Of course somebody will be going the same way.*

She stopped and pretended to look into a shop window, glancing into the glass behind her. She noticed a couple that stuck out from the locals—so obviously American it bordered on the absurd. They were middle-aged, decked out in sunglasses and hats, and even though she couldn't quite see their faces, Brook decided they were looking right at her. She walked on, taking a few zigzag turns into unknown side-streets, but never quite venturing down a dark alley. The couple kept following, matching Brook's pace step for step.

Entirely by accident, Brook found herself on another main thoroughfare with a great deal of traffic, both pedestrian and vehicular. A policeman stood by on the corner, directing cars when needed, and otherwise just watching. When she drew near him, Brook stopped suddenly and whirled on the people following her.

"Why are you following me?" she demanded, loud enough for the policeman to hear. "Who are you? Who do you work for?"

"You're Brook Burlington, aren't you?" the woman asked timidly. She was older than Brook had first thought, and by the accent, not American, but Canadian. She held Tom's book in her hand.

"Yes," Brook admitted warily.

"Oh my Lord!" the woman nearly swooned. "What are the chances of that, Harry?"

She was speaking to her husband, who just stared at Brook open-mouthed.

"We saw you coming out of the shop! I said it was you, and Harry said 'No, it can't be,' so we decided to follow you to be sure. We didn't mean to scare you."

"Would you autograph our book?" the man asked finally, coming out of his daze.

"I...it's Tom's book," Brook said, hearing an edge to her voice she hadn't intended.

"Please?" the woman said hopefully.

Reluctantly, Brook did as they asked.

*　　*　　*

It was another long shot, but Brook just had to try. From her father's writings and some of the documents within the shotgun, she'd come across the name of the man she believed had helped box up and ship the material she'd found in her mother's attic. The man's last known address was within walking distance; if it turned out to be a false lead, she needed a walk anyway.

When she arrived, she was surprised to see that the house was still there, and his family still occupied the place, but the man she had wanted to see had since died, and his relatives had nothing left that had belonged to him beyond a few pictures and their memories.

"He was a simple workman," they explained. "For a brief time, he worked for your father, which was the highlight of his life, and he often spoke of it fondly, but he did not read well, nor write. There are no records, no diaries. Nothing like that."

Brook thanked the family profusely and headed back to the hotel, refusing their offer of dinner. To her disappointment, even here, in an impoverished back road of Amman, Brook and her discovery were well known, and the family considered their connection to her a great honor.

On her walk back to the hotel, Brook's phone rang.

"Professor Green," she answered, noting the I.D.

"I've got something for you," he said.

"That was quick," Brook remarked.

"Yeah, it only took a second for my expert to spot the Russian royal seal on that book-cover you sent me."

"So that confirms it?" Brook answered, unable to contain the excitement in her voice.

"Sounds like it. He said he could just make it out on the copy, and showed me; it looks like some sort of two-headed bird."

Brook laughed.

"I think it's an eagle, Professor," she remarked.

"What do I know?" Green joked. "I'm old, I'm retired. Anyway, he says he'd need to see the book to be sure; there are tons of counterfeit seals around, but that this one looks like it's from the middle of the sixteenth century during the reign of Ivan the fourth—the terrible one, but they were all terrible, weren't they?"

Brook laughed again. Green was friskier than she remembered him. She wished she could fish out the book and study the cover again, but the streets were crowded and her hands were full with copies of Tom's book.

Better wait till I get to the hotel, she thought.

"My Greek chap hasn't got back to me yet," he went on. "That'll be the real proof. If this just turns out to be a translation of *Catcher in the Rye* or something...well..."

"Okay, Professor, let me know," Brook told him, not wanting to think about that scenario. "And thanks."

They said their goodbyes and hung up. Approaching the hotel, Brook thought she saw the Canadian couple enter ahead of her, but pushed down the uneasy feeling that rose in her stomach on sight

Why are you worried? Is it reasonable or paranoid?

Suddenly they were in front of her, crossing to the elevator.

"Oh, hello," the woman said, whirling towards Brook with a grin. "You're not following us, are you?"

Brook chuckled politely as the elevator arrived. Politely, she tried to sidestep the pair.

"Come join us for dinner," the woman blurted enthusiastically, blocking Brook's way.

"Yes, please," the man chimed in. "We're big fans."

"You know, I can't—" Brook sighed as the elevator left.

"We'd be so honored," the woman pressed. "We'll treat you, of course."

"It would be such a big deal for us," the man stated flatly. Brook wondered privately if anything had ever truly been a big deal to him.

"No, I'm sorry. Some other time—"

Another elevator came, and the woman grew frantic

"Just a drink then, in the lounge right over there. Fifteen minutes."

The woman was insistent, and Brook didn't like to be rude, but shook her head. She was beginning to worry about how desperate they seemed.

"Coffee?" the man suggested.

"No, thank you. I need to get up to my room; I'm expecting a call."

"She's a busy woman, Harry," the woman said to her husband haughtily. "She doesn't have time."

"A selfie, then?" Harry pleaded, pulling out his phone and stepping right next to Brook without waiting for an answer.

"Sure, okay," she answered, not being given much choice in the matter.

Another elevator came and went as Harry's wife squeezed in beside her, and the couple grinned into the phone like they'd known Brook Burlington their entire lives. The usual fumbling with the camera app followed—"Is it charged?"

"Did you push the button?" "Is this it?" "Did you save it?"— then the woman had to take a photo with her own phone "just to be sure", but Brook finally managed to get on the elevator and up to her room. Immediately, she knew something was wrong.

17

Brook's room had been searched, though 'ransacked' was more like it. Appalled, Brook closed the door silently, backed into the hall and hid, watching. The closet and bathroom doors had been closed, and she hadn't dared to look inside.

Trying to steady herself, she dialed a number. "Tom?"

"Hey, Brook, what's up?"

"Somebody broke into my room and went through my things."

"Ah, no! I'm so sorry. Did you call the police?"

"I called you first. I think there might still be somebody in there."

"Where are you now?" he asked, suddenly worried.

"I'm down the hall."

"Get out of there, Brook. Go down to the lobby. Don't tell them at the desk; just call the cops. The hotel won't want the police to come, so they'll try and cover it up. Hang up now, call the cops, and wait for them in a safe place."

To Brook's relief, the police came quickly—there were two of them, but only one spoke English. They accompanied Brook upstairs and pronounced the room empty after checking the closet and bathroom.

"They took my laptop computer," Brook told them after a brief inventory. "And some clothes."

The policemen gave each other a quick look, but didn't say anything.

"Do you know who did this?" the policeman who spoke English asked matter-of-factly.

"Not exactly," she said, not sure whether she should mention her earlier suspicions.

"Is anybody following you or bothering you? A man, maybe?" the policeman pressed, sensing Brook's hesitation.

"There was a couple," Brook began. "They said they were Canadian, but the more I think about it, the husband was faking it. They followed me when I was walking around the city, and they were here when I got back. They wanted to get a picture with me."

Brook paused. There was nothing sinister in that as she explained it, she knew, but something had been off.

"You are a celebrity," the English-speaking policeman said simply. "It's not always easy being a celebrity."

"Russian!" Brook blurted out, suddenly recalling her earlier encounter. "He was Russian. When he couldn't get his phone to work, he muttered something in Russian; it sounded like 'bleen'. I've heard other Russians say it, it's a curse-word of some kind.

They must have been sent to stall me! They stopped me coming up too fast; they wanted to have dinner or coffee, and when that didn't happen, they distracted me with pictures."

Brook gasped as realization hit.

"They took my picture! Several pictures. Oh my God!"

The policeman who spoke English looked up from his notebook.

"Did you take *their* picture, by some chance?" he asked.

A wave of panic bloomed from Brook's shoulders, and she suddenly felt as if she were standing on the narrow ledge of a tall building; the same way she'd felt that night at home after her encounter with her father's ghost in Woodburn Hall.

"Miss?" the policeman asked worriedly, bringing her back to the matter at hand. He probably wouldn't catch her if she fell. She needed to be strong.

"What was the question again?" Brook asked, turning her back on him and finding the edge of the bed.

"Did you take their picture, by some chance?" the policeman repeated.

"No," Brook answered flatly. "They used their phones; they have my face, I don't have theirs. I thought I was just being paranoid."

"But you would recognize them again if you saw them?"

"Absolutely."

"Okay," the cop said, putting his notebook away and giving her a card with his number on it. "If you see these tourists again, call me. Do you have the serial number of your computer?"

"I can get it. I have a record."

"Call me with that, and I'll add it to my report. Also...the clothes?"

"Pajamas. White with little red hearts, and a light blue pair."

The man wrote her description down, all business.

"I would change room," he suggested.

"Right away," Brook replied as she thanked him and showed them out.

Maybe I need another hotel altogether.

As soon as she was alone again, she called Tom back.

He picked up quickly. "Are you all right?".

"I'm fine," she replied, kicking herself as soon as the words left her mouth. She wasn't fine; she was having another nervous breakdown in a foreign country, and not exactly one she'd pick to do it in.

As if reading her thoughts, Tom replied, "I'll fly back to Amman tonight."

"No!" Brook protested sharply, again regretting the word the moment she heard herself say it. Of course she wanted him there with her; she couldn't face this alone.

"Okay..." he answered slowly, cowed by Brook's outburst.

"I'm fine. I really am," she said as calmly as she could. "They took my laptop and a couple of pairs of underwear, but I think that was just for show."

"For show?" Tom asked, not sure what that meant.

"To put the cops off the scent." Brook replied. "It was the laptop they wanted. I know there are a couple of Russians posing as North Americans involved, but they had help, of course. I need you to snoop around and see why the Russians are after me; we need to know whether Strelov is involved."

"Okay."

"Figure out who sent us those canopic jars as well, would you? It could be key."

"Got it," Tom answered.

"I'm going to give you a password, and then I'm going to email you a web-address for online storage. There's a file called 'insurance' on the account; I need my laptop model and serial number to give to the police."

"No problem."

"When I settle, I'll tell you what hotel I've moved to," Brook sighed. "Though I don't imagine it'll do much good if the Russians are on my tail again..."

"You're sure you don't want me to come back?"

"I'm not sure of anything," Brook admitted. "Oh," she whispered, lowering her voice, "by the way, I still have the book. Professor Green checked with some of his Russian history chums and they say it might be the real thing from you-know-where."

"Say no more!" Tom replied brightly.

The excitement in his voice almost brought Brook to tears. They both loved the archeological world so much. *This* was what was important to them, maybe more so than each other, and that knowledge was a tragedy Brook could never fully deal with.

18

Ankara, Turkey

His name was Ferhad Adab. His misfortune, and the reason he hung in the cold cell—his wrists, pulled to the ceiling by a strong chain, causing him excruciating pain and destroying his shoulder joints—was being the first cousin of Pejna Barzanji, Kurdish freedom-fighter.

Ferhad himself was no warrior. He drove trucks, cars, anything with wheels, and loved his work. It just so happened that one day he'd picked up a man whose name he never knew, a mid-level official of the Kurdistan Workers' Party. The PKK had been deemed a terrorist organization by the Turkish Government and targeted for extinction throughout the Middle East. The man Ferhad had been driving did not survive the assassination attempt when it had struck right in the heart of Sirsenk, situated in the autonomous Kurdish region of Iraq near the Turkish border. Ferhad did survive—on purpose, it turned out; he possessed information the Turks were desperate to know.

Mehmet Davidoglu, a member of Turkey's National Intelligence Organization—MIT—did the honors.

Ferhad had been awake for 72 hours, having spent most of it in one position or another designed to break bones, ligaments, muscles, nerves, and his spirit. Throughout it all, he had surprised himself with his own stubbornness. He'd always considered himself a weak man, averse to pain and unable to question authority, but Mehmet's cruelty was a great teacher of endurance, it seemed. Hatred welled in Ferhad, and the increasing agitation with which Mehmet applied each weapon of pain only steeled his resolve to endure every degradation, agony, and humiliation.

He should have known, of course. They wouldn't be content with just breaking Ferhad's body and spirit; they would go after his family as well. They were his reason for living; the source of all his joy, and very root of his incessant, mercenary striving, and long hours spent exhausted on the road, but also his greatest weakness. Mehmet had him.

"You will speak now, my friend," Mehmet whispered into the man's ear, "or we will go to your home with twenty men who will take turns raping your wife, your two daughters, and your son. Then they will be killed, and you will watch."

Mehmet waited.

Ferhad thought for a moment before giving a single weak nod.

"Yes," he managed to rasp. He'd had no water in hours, and before that no food, and before that they'd poured gallons of filthy sewage down his nose and throat until he was sure he would drown. "Yes, I speak."

For the first time in his unlucky life, Ferhad had much to tell. His cousin Pejna had returned from Amman telling of a lost treaty between the British Crown and the nascent Kurdish state of 1918, agreeing on the foundation of a geographical entity that had turned out to be no more than a wish thanks to the Turkish.

"I don't know if it exists," Ferhad moaned through swollen lips, his tongue dry from lack of water. He tried desperately not to cough as he spoke; if he started, he feared he would never stop. "I have never seen the document. Nor has Pejna; it would do no good to ask her. If you do, I will haunt you from the grave, and go after your wives, your mothers, and your children—"

A swift kick to Ferhad's face stopped that path of discussion. He choked a humorless laugh as a tooth and a mouthful of fragments tinkled on the stone floor. He wasn't sure he was physically able to speak anymore. A cough burned his throat, threatening to choke him.

It would be funny, he thought, *if they never got the information they were looking for because of their cruelty.*

"Go on," Mehmet coaxed. "Who has this treaty?"

"It's not a treaty," Ferhad heard himself correcting Mehmet. "It is a rough draft; a framework. A list of negotiating items between the two parties."

"Who?" Mehmet repeated.

"Brook Burlington."

There was no need to repeat the name; Mehmet had heard of her, and thought to himself that Ferhad's claim made sense. *She's no stranger to digging around in what she shouldn't.* Without a further word, he clapped his hands and dismissed the interrogators. They'd put in a great deal of overtime and missed lunch, and now they had what they needed, there was no hurry; they could come back for Ferhad later. If he was dead when they returned, they would take care of it then, and if he was still alive, well, they'd take of that too. Soon, Ferhad Adab would disappear from this Earth. It didn't matter how.

Pleased with his accomplishment, Mehmet left work early and returned home to his own family—a wife, and five daughters, aged four to sixteen. Other fathers would have found so many daughters onerous; but Mehmet considered them a blessing, a gift.

The girls rushed him when he walked into his comfortable, nicely furnished living room. The house was hardly a mansion, but it was sizeable, situated in a fashionable section of Ankara. Mehmet was not related to the current administration, but as keeper of their secrets, he held enough power to be considered a close associate— a *consigliere,* as the movies would have it—and rewarded accordingly.

"You are neglecting your homework!" Mehmet protested with a laugh as he embraced each girl.

The girls would gather in the living room in the afternoons and do their 'homework', spreading out their books on the couch, the floor, and the coffee table. As a seeker of truth and one of the Middle East's great interrogators, Mehmet knew a scam when he saw one—much of their conversation, he knew, was not math, science, or literature, but gossip, fashion, and romance.

And money—they were always pleading for money to go here or there or buy this or that, and he always gave it to them, no matter how many times his wife, Katife, asked him not to.

On permission to do things, however, Mehmet was far stricter. His was a secular world in an Islamic nation, and there were small things he permitted his daughters to do, and slightly out-of-the-way places he allowed them to go that many would frown upon, so he was careful for the reputation of the family and his standing in the government. For now, at least, Mehmet was fairly lenient—at least his daughters were asking permission. He hoped it would continue even as they grew older.

Katife floated into the room and joined the girls in embracing the man of the house. Mehmet thought she was as lovely as the day he married her, and often told her so, to which she would merely giggle girlishly. Lately, Mehmet had detected a note of sarcasm in that giggle, and had commented on it. She had turned the tables on him, accusing him of suspecting treason everywhere, even in his own home. On the surface, Mehmet had chuckled at the thought, pretending she had been joking, but in his heart he felt wounded, and considered it a horrifying omen that maybe this paradise—his household, his family—would soon end.

For this evening, fresh off of his success with the Ferhad investigation, everything was back to normal. Supper was delicious—the new cook was talented—and afterwards, the girls showed Mehmet what they'd learned in school that day, which was his favorite evening pastime. Though he hoped his daughters would eventually find husbands, have children, and enjoy rich family lives similar to the one he offered them, he was an enlightened man when it came to a woman's role in society and the workforce. He understood the importance of raising strong, independent women who could achieve anything they wanted for themselves.

The phone rang after three of his daughters had gone to bed, and Mehmet answered quickly so they wouldn't be awakened. It was his superior. His habit of calling Mehmet at home after hours irked the lower-ranked employee, but he would never dare to mention it.

"I want you to find this archaeologist you have uncovered," the man ordered without pleasantries, "and make sure what he's after never sees the light of day."

"Yes sir, that was my intention, sir," Mehmet answered, not bothering to correct the man on Burlington's pronouns. "About my request—?"

"Granted. Absolutely. You'll have a team of five, and your pick of men. If you are successful, there will be a promotion and a posting of your choice."

"I'm very happy here, sir," Mehmet replied.

The boss grunted.

"Very political. Don't lay it on so thick, will you? If you fail..."

There was no need to finish the sentence; Mehmet knew if he failed, there would be blood enough to fill the Hagia Sophia, the Bosphorus, and the cave cities of Cappadocia.

"I understand, sir," Mehmet said simply, trying not to let his fear bleed into his tone.

"Good. I'm pleased."

Before Mehmet could reply, the boss hung up.

He stood stunned, still holding the phone. He was a huge success, and everything he'd asked for, they'd given him, so why was he so scared? Why was his hand shaking?

19

T.E. Lawrence knew how important secrecy would be to this mission. To that end, he had enlisted Major Edward William Charles Noel in the enterprise, which he wrote in his diary was "nothing less than figuring out the post-Ottoman landscape in the vast political minefield that was the Middle East."

Noel's reputation as a trusted spy was known by only a small group, and an even smaller handful were aware that he'd just smuggled Tsarist General Peter Polovstov and his wife from Soviet Russia by disguising them as American missionaries.

Lawrence felt it was appropriate that they meet in Aleppo, one of the oldest continuously inhabited cities in the world. It was slightly off the beaten path, but not so out of the way that the presence of dignitaries would be particularly noticeable. He hoped to get an agreement signed between the various factions before their positions hardened, red lines were drawn, and ultimatums declared. There'd been too much war already, he felt, even though he'd been one of the fiercest fighters during it. The Great War had ended, yes, but the Middle East hadn't gotten the memo.

The rebels called themselves the Society for the Rise of Kurdistan. Everyone knew what they wanted—their own autonomous state—but no one was willing to give it to them; with the exception of Lawrence, who felt—along with Noel and a few other British and French diplomats—that Kurdish self-rule was the key to future peace in the area.

King Faisal, kicked out of Syria by the French and having secured his hold on Iraq, wasn't about to put his head in a noose by giving the Kurds a homeland north of Baghdad. Neither the Syrians nor the Turks were likely to give up territory, either—too much blood had been spilled.

If compromise was in the offing among the great powers, there would be a European-enforced carving up and division of Kurdish land between Turkey, Syria, and Iraq. Kurdistan would not exist.

It was a moving target, Lawrence knew, but he felt that an agreement might be reached if done in private, and without old hatreds being exhibited in long-winded speeches in public places and on the floors of various parliaments. With any luck, if things were executed properly, the Kurds would have their territory, which would stabilize the entire region—Turkey, Syria, Iraq, and even Persia.

Lawrence considered the very gathering of the representatives a minor miracle even before discussions began. He'd had to convince the principals of the need for secrecy, as well as to agree to attend without any preconditions or preconceptions of what might occur.

To Lawrence's consternation, the small delegation from the Society for the Rise of Kurdistan arrived with a list of demands written in English, French, and Arabic, declaring a free Kurdish state and demanding the full support and recognition of all the other powers in attendance, including the British Crown.

Lawrence and Noel were on thin ice. They pretended to represent the British government, but they truly had no idea how far their countrymen and ruler would support them. On top of that, the stakes were enormous. In private conversations, Noel had already noted that the Kurds could threaten British interests as well.

"No, no, they would counterbalance the Turks," Lawrence argued, "Faisal and Syria as well. Not to mention create an extra buffer zone between the region, the Caucasian 'stans', and Mother Russia."

After a week of arguments, sidebar negotiations, shouted insults, and walking off in a huff, a document was produced. It was miles away from granting all of the Kurds' demands, but provided them with one hope for the future; an autonomous state. Translations were made into English, French and Arabic—Italian would come later, it was decided—and the delegations all signed it—"a true miracle!" Lawrence declared—but it was understood that each of the delegates would need to take the agreement back to their respective governments for ratification. Right now, it was a legal pact, a chance for peace, but also a ticking time bomb that could explode at any moment. Everything would have to be agreed to in the darkness. Secrecy was paramount.

Lawrence had no illusions about how far out on a limb he had ventured in assuming the attitudes of his country to match his own, or how easily the Foreign Office, the Prime Minister, or even King George V himself could lop that limb off, but he also rejoiced at the accomplishment.

Noel and Lawrence shared a final drink after rolling the documents up and pushing them into the shotgun he'd received as a gift a year earlier from Isa bin Khalid bin Isa Huwaytati. Lawrence would attempt to deliver the precious manuscript to the authorities in British Egypt, moving across Arab territories occupied by armies that Lawrence had once advised.

20

Amman, Jordan

It was the change of hotel rooms that put her over the edge, Brook believed. She had waited until it was dark and kept the secret of her plans to herself.

If I don't speak, if I don't communicate outside my head, no one will know, her sane stream of consciousness explained to the other thoughts racing toward madness within her brain.

Even the simple routine of finding another place to stay, packing her bags, catching a cab out front and checking in elsewhere had become overwhelming, challenging her ability to cope.

Normally, she would have gone to the front desk and asked, "Would you please find me another hotel? No, there's nothing wrong with this one, I just need a change", but as she had locked eyes with the smiling receptionist, Brook had hesitated, and the panic set in.

What if the clerk here is in cahoots with the Russians? He'll book me into another place and they'll be over there ahead of me installing listening devices, cameras, and who-knows-what!

Suspicious, Brook had instead chosen to sneak out a side door in the middle of the night with a pair of suitcases, hailed a cab, and asked the driver to take her to the best hotel he could think of that was at least ten miles away.

It had taken three tries. The first place was fully booked, and the second place just looked dangerous. In desperation, Brook had called Pejna, hoping she could stay with her again—that was what Brook really wanted, to be safe with a friend—but there was no answer. In fact, Pejna seemed to have fallen off the face of the Earth since Brook had left her in the hotel lobby to go and meet with the bookseller. Brook had emailed, texted, and called her cellphone to no avail. She fleetingly considered going to Pejna's apartment to check on her, but that seemed desperate, and the other woman worked such long hours it would be cruel to wake her up in the middle of the night. Besides, her disappearance with no more than a text had made Brook wonder just how close they were anyway, and whether she had overstepped her boundaries by soliciting the poor woman's help with such a personal issue in the first place.

"Pejna, I hope you're happy somewhere with your children and their father," Brook muttered in the back of yet another taxi.

"Excuse me miss?" the driver asked.

"Nothing," Brook shot back, momentarily completely unaware of where in the world she was. She knew only that it was night, and she was alone. Just as it looked like she'd end up on an Amman corner with her suitcases and a suicidal despair mixed with paranoid fear, Brook found a hotel that would take her in, one with a soft bed and a hot bath. It lacked a few comforts, but there was no need for Wi-Fi; her computer was gone. She hadn't had to call her brother again; at least she'd avoided *that* humiliation.

Needing to hear a familiar voice that wouldn't pass judgement, Brook called Katy instead.

"Well, speak of the Devil!" Katy answered cheerfully.

Relieved, Brook started to laugh and cry at the same time.

"You there?" Katy asked, hearing only sniffles on the other end of the line.

"I'm here," Brook nodded.

"Where exactly is that?"

"Amman, Jordan."

"Are you all right? I've been worried about you."

"I'm a mess," Brook admitted.

"I'll book a flight right now. Tell me where you're staying. I'll drop Saqqara off at your brother's—the girls will be thrilled."

"No, no, don't. I don't want you to do that. I don't want you here," Brook told her friend.

"Hey, I can take a hint." Katy joked, unhurt.

"You know I didn't mean it that way. You've got other things to do, film festivals and all that. How's that going, incidentally?"

"It's going great, but they want you there, not me," Katy said. "What if I come to Jordan and film the sequel?"

"No thank you."

"'The discoverer of ruins breaks down herself'— it's catchy, don't you think?" Katy said.

"Not funny," Brook replied flatly.

"Too soon?"

"Way too soon."

"Is Tom there?" Katy asked.

"No, he's in Moscow doing some research."

"Call him. He'll love that. Men need to be needed, bless their little hearts."

"No, I won't," Brook said firmly.

"Does he know how much trouble you're in right now?"

"I think so."

"Then he'll be there soon. You can count on it."

*   *   *

Sure enough, Tom arrived the next morning. He said he'd done all he could in Moscow, but Brook didn't believe him. She was grateful for the lie, however, and loved him all the more for it.

Why is it honesty is never appreciated, Brook wondered, *but a caring, considerate lie is so endearing?*

Brook wasn't completely honest with Tom, either. She hid the full extent of her breakdowns; both this most recent one and the one before; and she didn't reveal her sleepless nights or nightmares about her father.

She brought him up to speed on the events she would allow him to know about, including the fake couple as they ate breakfast in her new hotel room.

"I wouldn't put it past the Russians to be tailing you," Tom agreed once she had finished.

"You mean I'm not paranoid?"

"No, I didn't say that," he grinned. "You could be paranoid *and* the Russians could be watching you."

"But why?" Brook mused.

"It could be you're onto something they're interested in, or it could be they just like to stick their nose in and make trouble. They've done that before."

While Brook thought about that and continued eating, her phone rang. After a quick glance at the ID, Brook knew it was her brother. Had Tom called him?

"Carl," Brook answered.

"Hey, Brook, how are you?" he asked. To her surprise, it sounded like he was offering a regular greeting and not a request for a medical briefing. Brook looked at Tom, whose eyebrows were raised in mild surprise—no, he hadn't called Carl.

"I'm fine," Brook lied. "How are things there?"

"All's good. Listen, your visa to Russia just came through."

Brook had forgotten about that. Tom seemed to be able to travel to and from Russia at will for some reason—Brook made a mental note to grill him about that later—but for her, such journeys meant a tedious process of visa applications, questions, and appearances at embassies. Carl had suggested the Burlington Foundation make the application on Brook's behalf, putting her travels down to foundation research.

"That was quick," Brook remarked.

"Yes, it was. I guess we have more pull with the Russians than I thought."

"Or they just want me in Moscow—"

"You're beloved the world over, Brook."

"—so it's easier to bump me off with their deadly poisons."

"Yeah, that's probably it," Carl agreed, laughing. "Any leads on anything?"

"Lots of leads, but they're going nowhere," Brook answered.

"Right. I'll email the visa information to you."

"Okay..." she answered hesitantly, thinking. She no longer had her computer, but there was always her phone, and Tom had brought his own laptop. Somehow, she'd get into her email.

"You'll have to go to the Russian embassy to pick up the actual documents, but they say they're all ready for you."

"Thank you, Carl. Thank you so much."

"There's one thing. It's only for a week, starting the day after tomorrow."

"What is?"

"Your visa. You have to be in and out of Russia in one week."

Brook sighed and ran her hands through her hair. "That's not enough time, Carl, you know that."

"That's the best I could do," he sighed. "They didn't even want to give you that long."

"I'm beloved all over the world—you just said that!"

"I was kidding!"

"That's not even the length of a tourist visa," Brook protested.

"I know, I know. But Tom will be with you, right? He can stay and press on while I work on wheedling them for a longer stay for you."

"Goodbye, Carl," Brook replied, hanging up on her brother before she was tempted to argue further.

The whole thing was maddening. What if instead of sticking her with some deadly radioactive agent, the Russians had already nailed her with something more slow-acting to drive her insane one day at a time, eating away at her brain cells, to cause a slow death, or perhaps early onset dementia?

"We've got to get you out of this room," Tom announced after a few moments, interrupting Brook's building paranoia.

"Good idea," she agreed. "There's a bookstore I want you to see anyway."

The new hotel was much farther away, and they were forced to take a cab. Tom wanted to talk; but Brook put her finger on his lips and shook her head towards the driver, who she didn't trust.

"Stop here," she ordered.

They were several blocks from the bookstore, as Brook had planned. She was hoping to shake any more 'Canadian tourists' or other nefarious characters.

"So is this where you found the book?" Tom asked, holding it tight in his jacket pocket. Brook had given it to him for safekeeping.

"That's right," she confirmed.

"I've been reading about your Tsar and his lost library," Tom said, making conversation as they walked. "Ivan the Terrible! More like 'Ivan the Maniac' if you ask me, though the Russians still like him for some reason. He killed his own son, but I guess that didn't count against you back then. He was a real bookworm, I noticed, a bibliophile. He demanded a vast dowry of books from his Byzantine wife, didn't he?"

"That was his grandmother, actually."

"What?"

"Ivan the Terrible's grandmother," Brook explained, "Sophia-something, the last Byzantine princess. She married Ivan the Third, Ivan the Terrible's grandfather, and part of the deal involved Sophia bringing a ton of reading material with her."

"Very romantic," Tom smiled.

"Yeah, he wouldn't sleep with her till all the books were on their shelves."

"I used to date a librarian like that," Tom joked.

"Very funny."

"So that's how the Lost Library got started?"

"That's what they say," Brook nodded.

"And you think this little number might have been a part of it." Tom tapped his jacket in the spot where the book was hidden.

"I don't know, but I'm being pointed in that direction."

"And it involves the Kurds?"

Brook shrugged.

"There's a lot I don't understand yet," she admitted.

21

Amman, Jordan

"Ah, I knew you'd be back!" the old bookseller called to Brook when she entered the shop. "And you've brought someone special with you, I see. It's not your husband; I know that."

Brook blushed as the bookseller thrust out his hand to shake Tom's.

"She told me she wasn't married, and I could tell right away she wouldn't lie about something like that."

"Oh, you never know," Tom replied nonchalantly, grinning at Brook.

"I can tell you she didn't believe anything I said, did you?" the seller accused, turning a wagging finger to Brook. "You didn't believe me the first time. You thought I was pulling the wool over your eyes."

He turned to Tom again. "Welcome to al-Nasrani's Books—I can see you are a more trusting soul."

"Like I say..."

"You never know, you never know," the bookseller laughed, shaking his finger at Tom now.

"You are al-Nasrani, then?" Tom asked.

"Pfft," the man said, waving his hand at the ridiculousness of it all. "Long dead, may Allah rest the man's soul. So, you are an archaeologist like the lady?"

It was Tom's turn to blush a little.

"No, I'm afraid not. An amateur at best, an *aspiring* archaeologist," he managed to say.

"Oh, I see," the man nodded wryly, as though this was code for something else that occurred between he and Brook.

"So, about that book you sold her..." Tom tried, turning the conversation to the topic at hand in an attempt to dodge the implication.

"Yes, the book," the bookseller said, an excited gleam in his eye. "Brought here by a young barefoot Jew when I was just a child myself."

"Do you know a man named Saleh?" Brook asked.

"I know many people," the shopkeeper protested, "but often I never learn their names. I don't know yours, for instance."

Brook and Tom realized that was true, but made no offer to correct it.

The bookseller merely laughed, finding that funny.

"What do you know about the Lost Library of Ivan the Terrible?" Tom asked.

With a smile still on his face, the seller replied, "I only know the stories. The Tsar hid his books in tunnels beneath his fortress in

Moscow so only he could read them. He had no interest in sharing them with the poor, starving people of Russia. When the Tsar died, his library was lost forever. Well, until our Jew traveler comes wandering in here to sell a book, and perhaps lead you two to its location."

Both Brook and Tom were stunned by the brash honesty of the statement.

"You recognized the seal on that book, didn't you?" Brook asked.

"I've wondered about its origins almost my entire life," the old man admitted, a tear coming to his eye.

A couple of customers entered the shop, making the bell chime above the door. The elderly bookseller, alarmed, gestured to Tom and Brook and spoke rapidly in Greek or Armenian, or perhaps it was only gibberish, indicating a certain aisle.

Brook took Tom's hand and pulled him along the narrow space between shelves. They heard the bookseller try and greet the new customers—two young European women, presumably tourists—in several languages, finally settling on French, which the bookseller spoke just as well as he did English.

"Sounds innocent enough," Tom whispered to Brook at the back of the shop. He was the language expert, though French was down on his list behind Japanese and Russian.

"Look," Brook remarked quietly, opening a linen-bound book that had been hand-written in a delicate Asian calligraphy. "This is Tocharian, I think."

"What's that?"

"An extinct language of the Tarim Basin in western China," she told him. "If I'm right, this is 7th Century; I should be wearing gloves. It's most likely Buddhist literature—"

The bell chimed as Tom and Brook heard the two women leaving. They prepared to return to the front when the bell rang again.

"Welcome!" the shopkeeper called to yet more new customers.

"Don't tell me—Canadian."

"You are right." The sound of the man's reply froze Brook in her tracks. There was a Russian edge to that voice which she recognized— it was the man who had wanted her signature...and her picture! Brook didn't wait to hear another word, or learn if the woman was with him for confirmation. She whirled and headed for the back with Tom in hot pursuit, not understanding anything but her panic. Miraculously, the two of them found a path through the piles of books to a back door—mercifully unlocked—then an alley and sunlight, leading to what they thought was safety.

22

Poland, 1946

Lev Abramovich's head pounded. He was vaguely aware of the motion that had awakened him; the shake of a boxcar rolling quickly over the rails. He'd been attacked—he remembered that. There'd been fists and boots and it had seemed useless to fight back, but his passivity hadn't reduced the violence; the blows had continued until Lev was out cold. There'd been several of them— he knew that much. He was now alone in the empty boxcar, with sunlight flashing through the rotted slats. The contents of his suitcase were strewn all over it.

"Wandering the wilderness," Lev muttered to himself just to be sure he was still alive. "Maybe this is how the Jews felt wandering the wilderness for 40 years."

As something nearby caught his eye, he laughed.

There it was, the book that had gotten him into so much trouble.

"People of the book, all right," he chuckled, picking up the ancient volume, warmed by the words he couldn't even begin to understand.

They'd taken everything except the book, the clothes on Lev's back, his worn blanket, and the suitcase itself, which they had destroyed by forcing it open. He checked the lining—yes, they had found the few Polish *złotych* he'd hidden there. Annoyed, he tossed the suitcase out the partly open boxcar door. The train was moving faster than it appeared to be, and he took solace in the possibility his attackers might have broken their miserable necks jumping off somewhere.

Lev held the book tightly, leaned against the wooden planks of the car, and watched the Polish countryside go by. For all he knew, he might be in Czechoslovakia by now, Hungary even. It didn't matter.

"Out of the frying pan and into the fire," he muttered to himself. It was an expression he'd adopted for himself throughout his twenty years of exile. Lev had heard there were refuges for Jewish displaced persons to the west, and had been heading there. When he had first heard of them, Lev had found the term hilarious, 'displaced persons'. That was him all right, displaced from Moscow since 1926, living on the run and hiding in the shadows with only the book to keep him company. It was the nearest thing to a family member he had left; the fate of his parents in Russia was unknown, and he had never dared to make inquiries. The last he saw of them had been on that frantic night.

Poland had been his destination afterwards, and he had brought with him the names and addresses of relatives. When the time came, he changed his mind, fearing the Russian OGPU would also know their whereabouts. Lev had instead memorized their names and addresses and made a point to avoid them completely. Even now, he remembered that night of interrogation vividly, and didn't want to visit that upon anyone, let alone his kin. Now it was too late, of course. He would never meet his distant cousins, aunts, and uncles—they'd all been taken away to the camps to die, and it had been all Lev could do to stay alive himself.

In his ten years of exile, Lev had come to recognize, albeit bitterly, the fact that the Special Section had done him a favor. Without them, and the fear they had instilled in him, Lev would never have gone on the run and or acquired the skills he had relied on so heavily to outlast the Holocaust.

Even now, as he sat and watched the morning sun flicker across the car, he realized that his attackers might have saved him—to go to a refuge now was impossible, even if he could manage to get past the "camp" designation of most of them. He had to remember that he was a Jew in hiding; whether from the Nazis or the Russians, it didn't matter as long as he was on the Soviet side of Europe. Regardless of who he was running from, he'd be shot, hanged or otherwise dispatched, Lev had no doubt. Death stalked him everywhere, and was constantly at his back.

He clutched the book even harder. Despite carrying it for over twenty years, he had never read it. He had meant to learn some Greek to do so, but the how or when that came with that ambition always eluded him. Even without understanding a word, he figured that he knew the contents after all this time. He guessed it was something philosophical; a dialogue between two fat, white-bearded Greeks in togas concerning the origin and meaning of the word "psyche".

Lev smiled at the fantasy. His academic education may have ended that night in Moscow, but he still retained enough knowledge of ancient history to get his imagination in trouble.

"Maybe your life is written in here," Lev mused, opening the book as he had a thousand times in recent memory. "Maybe your fate, everything that will happen, is here. A book full of signs; easy to read if you know how, but you don't."

Lev laughed again. He was becoming giddy, insane. He'd seen it in others too many times not to recognize it himself. If exile, a world war, and the wiping out of his people weren't enough, he was slowly losing his grip on reality. Pushing away the thought, he inspected the grazes and bruises that dotted his arms thoughtfully

"You've been beat up before," Lev told himself. "You'll be all right."

23

Tom and Brook ran for their lives down the Amman alley. As she pushed through small crowds of people, Brook glanced back at the shop. The man she had heard was indeed the Russian man, but the woman wasn't with him this time. In her place, there was another man, even larger than the first. By the way they held their hands inside their jackets, Brook guessed they were both armed.

"This way!" Tom shouted, pulling Brook down another small street, this one even less populated than the alley they had come from.

"Why this way?" Brook shouted back. It was just like a man to be giving directions to a city he'd never been in before.

"I don't know why!" Tom screamed. Ahead of them, a woman stepped out to block their way, and with her was another man. They, too, had their hands in their pockets—

Brook and Tom skidded to a stop. They were trapped, surrounded by people waiting at both ends of the street. There were no side streets, doorways, or unlocked gates to escape through—just unyielding stone walls on every side, a stone pavement under their feet, and the tiniest sliver of blue sky far above their heads.

"What do you want?" Brook shouted.

There came no reply, only a steady advance on both ends. She realized too late that it was a pincer move she and Tom were soon to be sandwiched in between.

Suddenly Tom was speaking Russian rapidly, with a strong, authoritarian voice despite the nervousness she knew he must have felt. In any other situation, Brook would have been annoyed at his tone; he sounded the epitome of the Alpha male barking orders to inferiors.

The quartet didn't bother responding, and just kept moving forward, tensing for violence. Brook hoped death would come quickly when they closed in. Their footsteps echoed on the cobblestones, but as she listened, Brook also became aware of another sound—a police siren, followed by the screech of tires and men shouting.

They came from both ends of the street behind the others—plainclothes cops or more gangsters cleverly disguised?

As soon as the quartet turned to look, Tom grabbed Brook and pulled her to the side against the wall. He shielded her as they knelt together, making them both as small as they could in case there was gunplay.

"Brook..." Tom whispered as they waited to die.

"I know." Brook replied.

There came no gunshots, just angry shouts in both Arabic, Russian, and Turkish—Brook was sure it was Turkish—followed by blows with fists and feet and maybe nightsticks. When she dared to look, Brook saw the four she assumed were Russians being roughly led away by a squad of a dozen men she hoped were plainclothes police she hoped. She didn't have to wonder for long; one of them was fast approaching.

"Are you Brook Burlington, archaeologist?" the man asked in perfect English from thirty feet away.

Brook wasn't sure what to say.

*   *   *

It didn't feel like they were under arrest. There were no guns, no handcuffs, and the men who had put Brook and Tom into the back of the shiny black car hadn't searched them for weapons or anything. On the other hand, neither of them had the feeling they were permitted to refuse, or argue with the instructions.

"What's this about?" Tom had asked, receiving only a shake of the head for an answer. "Who were those people?" he had tried, "Who are you?"

Again, there was nothing.

"Just come with us, please," the man with the perfect English told them.

To their surprise, the car had taken Tom and Brook back to the new hotel, and fresh anxiety started to build in her stomach—she had told no-one about the move, had they followed her?

A man who introduced himself as Mehmet Davidoglu was waiting for them, sitting at the small writing desk in Brook's room.

Brook didn't bother to ask how he'd gotten in. By the looks of things, he'd been going through Tom's computer following a search of the room.

Mehmet stood, dismissed the guards, and suggested Tom and Brook take a seat on the bed.

They obeyed, more curious now than alarmed. If they were going to be killed and their bodies dumped by the side of the road somewhere, it would have been done already.

"You probably know what this is about," Mehmet began. He spoke English well, not at a native level, but close.

Must have gone to an American university, Brook decided.

"No, we have no idea why we were kidnapped." Tom replied.

Mehmet laughed.

"Not kidnapped. Rescued. I assure you, those Russians would not have been as gentle."

"What do you want?" Brook asked, her courage building now that her fear of imminent death had faded a little.

"I want what you want," Mehmet stated cryptically.

"You'll have to be more specific than that," Brook shot back.

"Peace; world peace. Isn't that what we all want?" Mehmet asked sincerely.

The conviction in his tone took Tom and Brook aback. They had expected him to be the type of person driven by money and greed, but this this man seemed alarmingly genuine and empathetic.

"Let me show you something," Mehmet said suddenly, as if a thought had just occurred to him. He reached into his pocket, and both Tom and Brook tensed and backed away a little, expecting a weapon.

Instead, Mehmet opened his wallet to reveal a photograph:

"My wife, Katife, and my five daughters."

Tom and Brook took a quick glance to be polite.

"No, really look."

Mehmet handed them his wallet for a closer look.

"They're lovely," Brook stated simply.

"Thank you. I think so, too," Mehmet replied. "Some men might find so many daughters a burden, but I know they're a blessing, a gift."

Tom sighed sympathetically and gave Mehmet his wallet back. He put it away carefully.

"The worst thing for me and my family would be war, you understand?" he asked.

Brook and Tom nodded hesitantly.

"We are Turkish," Mehmet sighed. "We are surrounded by war, but except for the occasional terrorist incident, which I know you have in your country as well, we have stayed at some sort of peace for over a hundred years. We lost our empire, yes, but we do have peace. You understand that could change at any moment?"

Brook began to see where this was going.

"You know what I'm looking for," Mehmet said urgently, his voice less friendly now. "I know there is some sort of agreement with the Kurds made long ago which could threaten the peace and stability of my country and my family—the whole region, in fact."

"I don't have anything like that," Brook insisted as forthrightly as she could. Technically, it was true; the document was far from the real thing.

Mehmet's expression hardened, and his features twisted in anger. Brook wondered if it was he who'd taken her laptop and searched her other hotel room the way he'd obviously searched this one. In that moment, he looked like he was going to order the two of them be strip-searched and tortured in some undisclosed hellhole until they came clean.

"But you're looking for this document, aren't you?" Mehmet smiled. It was a funny grin, full of teeth, like the forced smile of a schoolboy who'd just learned the dictum "you'll catch more flies with honey than vinegar".

"I don't know," Brook answered. "I try to dig without any preconception of what I'm going to find. I let the evidence tell me."

Mehmet laughed.

"Very good!" he exclaimed. "Spoken like a true academic, yet completely ridiculous!"

"Wait a minute—"

Mehmet held up his hand, and Tom fell silent. He was still in charge, no matter how much fun he was having. "All I'm asking," he went on, "is that *when* you find this dangerous truckload of documentary dynamite, you turn it over to us, the rightful owners, in the interest of world peace."

"I won't promise that," Brook replied defiantly.

"'No justice, no peace', right?"

Brook wasn't sure what he was insinuating.

"I know you have a friend," he said. "Pejna, right? Pejna Barzanji? She's a lovely woman, very brave, a real credit to her murderous tribe. She has two children of her own, I believe."

He didn't need to go on—he could see the horror the veiled threat brought to Brook's face.

"Just let me know," Mehmet said, standing and offering both Tom and Brook his card. "Call me, or just scream—my men won't be too far away, I assure you. I know you'll find what you're looking for; I've been told you're very good at what you do. I also assure you that you'd rather deal with us than with those pesky Russians. They ran you ragged on the Cleopatra adventure, didn't they?"

Mehmet laughed again, even more pleased when Brook and Tom didn't.

"I'm so glad we had this little talk," Mehmet concluded brightly. "Have a nice evening."

As quickly as they had been brought to him, he was gone.

Tom rushed to his computer to be sure all his files were still there. Satisfied, he turned up the sound and played some music, loudly, just in case Mehmet and his Turks had left a listening device.

"You still have the book?" Tom whispered under the heavy bass beat.

Brook checked. Yes, the mysterious Greek book was still there.

"It's a lucky thing they didn't search us," Brook exhaled excitedly.

"Yes, it is," he agreed, slipping a book out from under *his* shirt. It was the linen-bound book handwritten in Tocharian that Brook had seen at the bookshop.

"For you," he said, handing it over with a flourish.

"You stole a book?" she gasped, thrilled and scandalized at the same time.

"Well, no——," he said awkwardly, "I just didn't get a chance to pay for it," and they both burst out laughing.

24

Amman, Transjordan, 1946

Lev wandered into Amman, Transjordan, searching for food, work, shelter, and a pair of shoes. It had been a year since World War II had ended in Europe, and still Lev wandered. There were many like him these days—lost, bewildered, and having endured untold hardships throughout the long war, yet surviving somehow. Some Jews—the ambitious ones with a little hope left in their bodies and souls— had thought of going to Palestine, where they might be safe. Lev Abramovich was one of them.

Lev arrived in Amman on Independence Day, May 25, 1946, when the country of Transjordan—eventually simply Jordan— was finally granted freedom from British rule. The noise, the celebration, and his own weakness from lack of food frightened Lev greatly, and when he found an alley to hide in, he stayed put until the next day, when the holiday was over and the people had returned to their normal jobs and normal lives.

A young boy sat behind the counter, ready and eager to greet the latest arrival to al-Nasrani's bookshop. He'd been given the responsibility a week earlier, when the bell above the door had fallen down and the youngster's father had declared it wasn't worth the trouble to nail it back up there.

"It scares the customers anyway," al-Nasrani had added, "and now that I'm a citizen of a free, independent state, I will no longer answer to a bell like a farm-animal."

Neither the boy nor al-Nasrani had anticipated what would walk through the silent door that day.

A ghost, the boy thought on first sight. The figure was whitish, with long, unkempt hair, and rags for clothes, that barely covered his bony, emaciated body.

Al-Nasrani was just as horrified as his son, and backed away a step, but the child knew his duty. He stood from his stool and marched to the front without hesitation. If the ghost wanted him dead, there was nothing he could do about it anyway.

"May I help you?" the boy asked in Arabic, which the ghost didn't seem to understand. He tried again, in English this time.

"I need to speak to the owner," Lev told the child in his own broken English, not sure if he would be understood.

"What for?" the kid answered, this time in fluent Russian, now confident of the ghost's country of origin. The boy had always been good with languages, and was a bit of a show-off about it, rattling off all sorts of things in all sorts of tongues.

"I have something to sell," the ghost replied in Russian, clearly more confident in a familiar language.

The boy worried that all the ghost had to sell was the worn pair of shoes hanging over his shoulder, for which he would be lucky to get anything. There were holes in the soles, and the laces had been knotted together so many times they looked like spider's nests. Sensing eyes on him, the boy looked for help. His grandfather and an uncle who had an uncanny nose for scandal and gossip now joined his father behind the counter. The three of them stared at the ghost with the same horror the boy felt.

"It's a book," the ghost told the boy, reaching into what was once a shirt and carefully half exposing a volume as if it were solid gold.

The boy's father signaled him to lead the ghost over.

"My name is Lev Abramovich," the man said in Russian, shaking his father's hand.

The boy hurried over to translate, and the haggling began.

*   *   *

With a full belly and shoes on his feet, Lev had thought he'd be able to think more clearly, but that wasn't exactly the case. He'd spent the last twenty-some years with the book next to his body, and through those long years he had checked every few seconds— both asleep and awake—to make sure the book was still there. Now it wasn't anymore, he felt like a man who had lost his foot, or an arm, but still felt pain in the missing limb. Lev still didn't know if the thing had been a blessing or a curse, but now it didn't matter, and there was no point in dwelling on it. He had needed to eat; another day without food would have been his last, he was certain, so the book...

"Had to go!" he shouted to nobody in particular. The train-yard was empty, it was the middle of the night. Only those like himself would be there now—derelicts, hobos, ne'er-do-wells. It didn't matter where he travelled; rough sleepers were the same the world over. Lev knew he should sleep himself, but he couldn't. He was too excited. He had asked around and figured out which train he should board. He had been told there was one that was loaded at dawn to head west to Jerusalem, Palestine. There were no empty or unlocked cars that he could see now, but Lev knew he could slip on board during the loading process—his rail skills had been honed over years of wandering.

All his life, Lev had heard the phrase "next year in Jerusalem". Now it wouldn't be a pipe dream; there was no wistful "next year", but instead, a definite "tomorrow in Jerusalem". His destination was only 90 kilometers west, Lev had been told, if he could manage to cross the border unseen— he was without papers, and had no idea where he would get them at this point in his life. The fact Jordan was now free of British rule struck him as an omen— occurring unbeknownst to him on the very day of his arrival in Amman—that Palestine would soon be rid of them as well, and a Jewish state established.

"What if it happens tomorrow?" Lev asked himself, giddy with his own power and freedom.

"Today the book, tomorrow Jerusalem, the next day Israel," he muttered alone in the night.

25

Moscow

As they entered the Moscow airport, and walked down the long exit past Customs, Brook and Tom spotted a driver with a sign that said, "Brooks Burlinton."

"A man without a 'g,'" Tom commented dryly.

"Did you order a ride?"

"Not me."

"He's seen us," Brook shivered, "He's coming our way."

"Miss Burlinton, Mr. Manor, I come from Mr. Strelov, who sends his regards," the man said as he approached.

Close up, the two travelers could see this was no ordinary driver. For one, he spoke perfect English, and for another, he had the body and face of a world-class boxer, with a clear bulge in his jacket in case his boxing skills weren't enough.

"Mr. Strelov is desperate to meet you both," the man went on.

"Where is he then?" Tom asked, making a show of looking around the terminal.

"He would like you to be his guests while you're in Moscow," the underling explained. "I will drive you to his *dacha*."

"No thanks," Tom said simply. He took his suitcase in one hand, Brook's hand in the other, and then headed for the exit.

It seemed the driver was an accomplished sprinter, too. He kept up with the couple through the terminal, calling after them. "I assure you there is no danger. Mr. Strelov is only interested in helping you. He would not harm either of you, believe me."

Tom and Brook had no intention of stopping, but the man was unfazed. "Why would he hurt you? After all, he gave you the canopic jars as a gift."

Coming to a stop in unison, they stared at the man, who gave them his most innocent look.

Tom looked to Brook. She was just as confused as he was.

"Conference," he told her, and stepped away from the driver, holding his hand out in the universal indication of 'private'.

"Don't tell me you're entertaining the thought of going with this thug!" Tom hissed when they were out of earshot.

"If we don't go to see him, we may never know what Strelov wants."

"The Cleopatra artifacts?" Tom suggested. "He tried to take them from you once, maybe he hasn't given up yet."

"Those are out of reach, absolutely," Brook assured Tom. "Anyway, I certainly don't have them, so it would take an army. We need to know why he sent the jars, A man like him could kill us the second he liked. If he wanted to, he would have already."

"Unless he wants to torture us first for information," Tom

retorted.

"What information? I don't know anything. You don't know anything—"

"Thanks."

"You know what I mean—anything of real value. You know those canopic jars are worth a quarter million each, right?"

"Really?" Tom asked, surprised.

" I don't know what he wants that's more valuable than those."

"Maybe he wants them back."

"Then we'll give them to him. I really don't care," Brook said.

"So you're saying 'yes'?" Tom concluded.

She nodded, and he sighed. Together, they made their way back to the driver.

"Okay," Tom stated sternly, poking a finger into the man's considerable chest, "but if we get killed, I'm going to blame you for it, you hear?"

"Please," the man said, thrilled at his success, "let me take your bags."

He grabbed their suitcases and ran with them to the car as if they were nothing.

It was an hour's drive to Strelov's *dacha*. Brook and Tom sat in the back of the oversized German luxury sedan and kept to their own thoughts, not speaking. The driver often glanced in his rear-view mirror, becoming more upset at the silence as the ride proceeded. There was no glass between the driver and his passengers; perhaps he had been hoping to overhear their conversation.

And shorten the torture required, Tom thought bitterly to himself as he observed this.

They looked out the windows at the city of Moscow, then at the countryside going by. Brook had been to Russia a few times, but Tom had lived there and spoke the language well. His experience matched her impressions now; Russia was a country of contrasts, with incredible beauty residing next to absolute despair.

She allowed herself to drift away, letting the motion of the car and the beauty of the forest and quaintness of the tiny villages that lined the roads transport her to another time, somewhere Medieval, edging towards the Renaissance.

Tom, on the other hand, stayed alert, memorizing their route and noting the signposts, certain he would have to drive them back to safety later, possibly in a broken-down, Russian-made two-door deathtrap—or perhaps a motorbike—with the whole KGB at their backs.

Eventually, they arrived at a prim, brightly painted *dacha*. A plump woman with squinty eyes, high cheekbones, and a loud, raspy voice came out to the car in a huff. Ignoring Tom and Brook, she proceeded to bark at the driver, who by his flinching seemed scared that the woman would beat him senseless.

Brook looked at Tom, hoping for a translation. His face stayed neutral. Perhaps this was their driver's wife, and he had forgotten to take out the trash?

The driver replied in quivering tones, which prompted a phlegmatic "humph" from the woman, though she seemed satisfied with the answer.

"You," the woman said to Brook, pointing at her as though she'd just been picked for some distasteful task. "You come with me, please."

Brook obeyed, and Tom took a step to follow.

"Not you," the driver told Tom, stepping in front of him to block his way.

Tom and Brook exchanged a momentary look.

"I'll be okay," she said, following the woman.

Tom, though frustrated, stayed put.

Brook admired the *dacha* as she walked through. It was quaint, cozy, and understated. As a vacation spot, Brook would have loved to stay here and unwind for a couple of weeks or months, especially if there were a few first-class chefs and a caring psychiatrist on staff.

It might be the answer to all your troubles, she thought.

Brook's trepidation returned, however, when the woman ahead of her suddenly stopped, signaling that Brook should do the same. The woman pressed a button on the hall wall, and after a couple of beats, a man and woman emerged from an adjacent room. Their dark blue uniforms reminded Brook of police, or prison guards. Crisply professional, the woman patted Brook down for weapons and listening devices while the man repeated the process with an electronic wand.

"If only they were this polite at the airport," Brook joked uncomfortably. There was no response; they apparently knew no English.

Or they're robots.

The final door was like every other one lining the way. The woman knocked and waited for an answer in Russian. She unlocked the door with a key, and then escorted Brook inside.

Strelov stood behind his desk with an enormous grin on his face, as if he and Brook were long-lost friends.

"So good to see you again, Miss Burlington," he said, taking her right hand in his and reaching to her elbow with his left in an apparent gesture of friendliness.

Or a jujitsu hold, Brook couldn't help thinking.

"You had a pleasant ride in from the airport, I trust?"

"Yes, very nice."

"I think you'll find the *dacha* quite pleasant as well," Strelov assured her. "I think you might be in need of relaxation, no?"

Brook didn't reply.

"Please, have a seat," he offered, indicating a chair.

Brook did as she was told. Strelov took an identical chair nearby, foregoing his desk. He offered wine, or something stronger, as well as something to eat. Still wary, she turned him down.

"Please relax," he said. "I am not detaining you or your boyfriend, I assure you, but we have so much in common, I thought we should talk."

Again, Brook said nothing. She couldn't imagine what she and Strelov could possibly have in common, except the Cleopatra tomb he had nearly stolen from her.

"You see, my grandfather and your father were both treasure hunters in their own way."

"Is that right?" Brook answered flatly.

"Yes, my grandfather was after something very interesting and very valuable."

"Did he find it?"

Strelov shook his head. "Unfortunately, no, but I believe he came very close. He ran afoul of the authorities and was sent to a labor camp in Siberia."

Strelov settled into his seat as Brook stared—was Strelov going to tell her his grandfather's life story?

"That's where my father grew up; in Siberia, near where they kept my grandfather. My grandmother moved with my father and his siblings to the town nearby. They would climb a hill overlooking the prison and wave to him every day for years, until my grandfather's death. It was a hard life, and at times my father felt the world was completely unfair—perhaps you know the feeling—but in the end, he was grateful for his experiences, because they toughened him and helped him survive in this world which can be so much trouble at times."

"A boy named Sue," Brook muttered.

Strelov looked puzzled for a moment then burst into that grin of his again.

"Johnny Cash!" he exclaimed, getting the reference. "You have it. Very good."

"Thank you."

"You see, you and I are very much alike," Strelov hurried on, sensing Brook's growing impatience with the discussion. "We have both lost relatives who left us with unfinished business, and we have both made it our life's mission to redeem them by fulfilling the missions they never succeeded in completing."

Brook shrugged—there was no point arguing with him.

"Your grandfather was a KGB agent as well, I take it?" she asked.

"Well, yes," Strelov admitted, taking the dig. "Of course, there was no KGB at the time, but he worked for a similar organization."

"And what was his 'life's mission?'"

"That's what I like about you Americans," Strelov smiled, getting up from his chair to glance at something on his laptop. "You have no filters, no shame or sense of decorum. You speak your mind. 'No bull'—isn't that your expression?"

"That's one," Brook replied guardedly.

"Just allow me to conclude my point," Strelov said quickly, sitting again. "You, my grandfather, your father—all of us, we all have the same trait; the urge to act on a single-minded obsession. Your pursuit of the Cleopatra and Antony tomb proved to me just how dedicated you can be, and how we might work together in the future."

"I don't think so."

"Not *together* as such—I don't mean that. My English isn't so perfect. I mean how we might be of help to each other. Beneficial. Like the canopic jars I gave you."

"You can have those back!" Brook offered brightly.

"I don't want them back. They're yours. A present. Possibly a wedding gift for you and Tom?"

"None of your business."

"Ah, direct again," he noted with a smile.

"I'm going to be even more direct," Brook told the man. "I know very well you're an experienced interrogator. You have probably done over a thousand of these interviews and know all the tricks of the trade. You'll start out pretending we're best buddies, then going hot and cold, all good cop/bad cop. I don't know, I'm not—"

"You'd like me to get to the point," Strelov interrupted.

"Yes, please."

"I will, as quickly as I can," Strelov told her. "I have a list. A 'bucket list', I think it has come to be called. A list of things I want to accomplish during my time on Earth. Finding the tomb of Cleopatra and Antony was first on that list, as you may imagine. You ruined that for me."

Strelov paused there, as though controlling his temper. He took a stroll around the room and opened a cabinet. Inside was a fully stocked bar.

"I think I will have that drink," he said. "Are you sure you won't join me?"

"No, thank you."

"Very well. I have been watching you ever since the Cleopatra episode. Your ability to find her impressed me greatly, since it had been my own desire as well. It made me think you might have sufficient skills to work with me on the second item on my list. It is an inherited project..."

"Your grandfather's project?"

"Yes—"

"Which is?"

Strelov held a finger up for Brook to be patient.

"That book, the one you purchased in Amman—"

"That *was* you, then? Your people following me?" Brook asked, not caring that she was interrupting him again.

"I plead guilty," Strelov said, holding up his hands. "You are a very interesting person, and I know you are always working on something, so I...keep track. My apologies. I only want to see the book."

"That was what that little walk around your desk was just about," Brook realized. "Somebody searched our luggage while I was sitting here."

"Again, my apologies."

"You know I don't have it, then. It's safely put away; you can't have it."

"Do you know what I do for a living?" Strelov asked. "Do you know the reason I can give away millions of dollars of priceless antiquities while spending many more millions searching for others?"

"I've been told you are an arms dealer," Brook said carefully.

"That is correct," Strelov told her. "But it doesn't mean I want to start wars around the world, no matter how good for business that might be. In fact, I have in my possession a certain treaty which might just make billions and keep my munitions factories operating day and night if it were made public."

Brook stared.

Just how much does this man know?

"I know quite a bit," Strelov said, reading her mind, "and I would rather have this treaty in your hands—hands I trust—rather than keep them in my own and risk being accused of exploiting war and causing death and destruction."

"What treaty are you talking about?" Brook asked, feigning ignorance.

Strelov laughed.

"Very good," he said. "You know which one, I believe you have an early draft. Mine is official, signed by the Foreign Minister of Italy and agreed to by the Prime Minister. It even has the government seal."

"It's in Italian?"

"That's right. It verifies that the treaty existed. It makes it real. That's what you want, isn't it?"

"It's not signed by Great Britain."

"Or France, that's true. You don't expect me to do all your work for you, do you? The point is," Strelov went on, "I don't want the thing. It smacks of war mongering, and despite my reputation, that's one bridge too far for a poor kid from the wrong side of the train-tracks in a Siberian wilderness to cross. No, what I'm looking for is something entirely different. One of the great mysteries."

"The Lost Library of Ivan the Terrible?" Brook suggested.

Strelov froze, giving it away—he couldn't help himself. He smiled sheepishly, and shook a finger at Brook.

"You're good. You're very good," he said.

"So you'll exchange the treaty for the book?" Brook realized.

Strelov smiled and nodded.

*   *   *

"He wants the book," Brook whispered to Tom once they were reunited.

Strelov had given them a beautiful suite on the second floor, overlooking the lush gardens and fishpond beyond. It would have been a perfect place to stroll and talk, and Brook wondered how many microphones had been planted out there versus how many were in the room.

Tom continued to unpack, and neither spoke further, both aware of the possibility of eavesdropping. After a few moments, he closed his case, held a finger up and took out his laptop, powering it up to play some good-old rock-n-roll just loud enough to drown them out. He put it on the bed, and he and Brook gathered around it like it was a fire on a cold day.

"They searched our bags, I think," Tom said.

"Yes, he told me as much."

His eyebrows shot up. "He *told you*?".

"Yeah, told me right out. He's shooting straight as far as I can tell; he put it all out there. He wants to trade the book for a copy of the treaty."

"The treaty?" Tom asked incredulously.

"That's right," Brook said. "Strelov says he has a signed treaty between the Kurds and the Italians—a formal version of the document in Lawrence's shotgun."

"How did that happen? Why didn't Lawrence deliver the papers?"

It was a good question, but neither of them had an answer to it.

"It's probably just a temporary strategy, this 'trade' thing," Tom warned severely. "I don't trust him one bit, and neither should you."

"I don't."

"But we're here, aren't we?" His tone took on a bitter edge, and he moved away slightly.

"Let's not fight. We need to stick together—"

"As long as you make all the decisions?"

"That's not what I mean, Tom, and you know it. It's just that after all is said and done, Strelov and I *are* similar people, with similar backgrounds."

"Dangerous to be around, you mean," Tom answered.

Brook laughed, grateful his joke had dissolved the building tension.

"Yeah, something like that."

"He *is* a dangerous man," Tom warned.

"Yes. Yes he is."

"And yet you're willing to play along."

"He's worried about starting a major war in the Middle East, and so am I," Brook said intensely. "You know what the last thing he said to me was?"

"What?"

"'You might be afraid of me, but you should really be afraid of the Turks.'"

Tom thought about that.

"He's right," he said finally. "He probably doesn't need another Middle Eastern war, and the Turks...they're as crazy about the Kurds as they are about the Armenians. They wouldn't hesitate..."

"They wouldn't hesitate to kill an archaeology professor to keep the Kurds off their backs," Brook finished the thought for him.

"They wouldn't think twice," Tom agreed gravely.

They leaned back on the bed for a few more minutes, the laptop between them.

"Do you think he put a bug in my computer?"

"No doubt about it."

"He's probably listening to us right now."

"You better shut it off," Brook suggested.

Wind of Change by the Scorpions filled the air.

"In a minute—I love this one," Tom remarked, holding up an imaginary lighter.

"I follow the Moskva, down to Gorky Park..."

Brook laughed.

"So how does the book get him the Lost Library? I don't understand," Tom admitted.

"No idea. He wouldn't explain."

"Where *is* the book, by the way?" Tom asked casually.

Brook shook her head. "It's better if you don't know."

"I could always tickle it out of you, you know."

"Probably, but you won't. You're quite the gentleman that way."

"Yeah, I know," Tom stated dismally. "So we're held hostage here until you hand over the book?"

"No. Not at all," Brook explained. "He offered to drive us back to our hotel in Moscow. I told him I *wanted* to stay another day."

Tom was startled. "Why?"

"It's beautiful here," Brook replied simply.

Tom nodded. It was. Smiling, Brook turned Sam and Dave up even louder.

"It's almost sunset," he remarked.

"Yes. Strelov said supper would be in about an hour."

"I bet it'll be tasty," Tom guessed, "...and laced with strychnine."

Brook laughed.

"Well, as long as it tastes good," she said.

"Brook, are you all right?" Tom asked. It was the first time he'd asked since they'd gotten back together. It was a legitimate question, and he was entitled to a full, accurate, honest answer....

"I'm fine," Brook heard herself say instead. Tom had seen the pills in her suitcase, no doubt. So had Strelov's people.

"Would you like to walk in the garden before supper?" he asked simply, taking her hand.

"That would be very nice."

26

Moscow

"There, that one!" Brook told the driver. "Stop here." She had picked a computer store at random in the upscale shopping district of Petrovka Street, Moscow.

"Come in and help me translate," she asked Tom.

He nodded.

"We'll just be a few minutes," Brook told the driver. They went inside the store and Brook bought a simple laptop, not quite the cheapest, but close.

"If I'm going to have these things stolen," she told Tom, "there's no use spending a lot of money."

"That's smart," Tom agreed. "And if somebody's going to bug it, maybe you ought to consider a laptop disposable anyway, like a burner phone."

Brook considered that as she paid for the device. If her computer hadn't been stolen and she'd had it with her the last few days, Strelov might have had it hacked anyway. All that was necessary was that the thing be somewhere in the vicinity of his wi-fi, right?

"There's a lot I don't know about things," she commented to Tom as they got back into the car.

"Stay loose," he had reassured her. "One step at a time."

Baby steps—that's what Dr. Green had called them when he moved to the shore, Brook remembered.

The driver dropped them off at the Moscow hotel, seeming very pleased with himself as he retrieved the bags from the back of the car.

"Hey, buy yourself something nice," Tom told the driver, and tried to slip some rubles into the man's pocket. The driver laughed and refused, as if giving a driver of his magnitude a tip was the height of absurdity.

The dated hotel was apparently as good as it got in Moscow, which made Brook wonder if it had been a mistake to refuse Strelov's offer to let them stay at the dacha a few days longer. It was the logistics that convinced her to say no. Their business was in Moscow and the *dacha* was just too far away. At best they'd have been beholden to the driver, who no doubt would be reporting their every move directly to Strelov. As it stood, Brook was sure they were being followed anyway, and who knew what kind of invasive surveillance was standard at a tourist hotel in Moscow?

She flipped open her laptop for the first time and got to work on the tedious process of setting it up and connecting her e-mail accounts. The messages were mostly the usual stuff, things she could answer later, or delete out of hand, but one e-mail caught

Brook's attention. It was from Pejna:

"Did you find what you were looking for? P"

Brook didn't know how to respond. *What did Pejna really know? Could she be trusted?*

"Not yet. B," Brook wrote back, keeping it brief. She felt terrible about shutting her friend out like this, but on the other hand the risks were just too great. She figured this is what spies had to live with every day: living dishonest lives, never revealing their true colors.

*   *   *

At lunch, Tom took out a large tourist map and made room on the table.

"Okay," he said, "let's say I'm Tsar Ivan the Terrible and I need to hide my books somewhere," Tom mused. "Where would I do that? Do we follow the Moskva down to Gorky Park?"

"Well the library is supposed to be underground," Brook commented, ignoring the joke.

"Okay, that's valid. Underground. Which means it's probably under the palace, no doubt, and nobody's going to let us into the palace to dig around in the floor."

"There has to be an entrance!" Brook said, playing along.

"Correct!" Tom over-did it, pointing at Brook with exaggerated flair. "Absolutely. We aren't looking for a library so much as an *entrance* to a library."

"Just like with Cleopatra and Antony."

"But in this case, there might be an exit as well," Tom reasoned. "If the Tsar wanted his library to himself, and he needed to be sure it stayed private and secret, he might have included a secret exit, right? A way out just in case."

Brook nodded hesitantly, not so sure.

Tom took out a pen.

"Okay, here's the Kremlin," Tom said. "There's not much left of it now, but that's where Ivan's palace was. It was rebuilt many times over the years, but the point is..." Tom drew a circle around the site he was referencing. "The point is since nobody in the Kremlin is going to let us in to look around the basement for secret passages, if there's another way out of the library, it might be here within this circle."

They stared at the map.

"Look here," Tom realized, pointing to the places where his line intersected the Moscow River between two bridges. "If there's a way in...it's here…" Tom drew a circle around a line on the north side of the river.

"It's worth a try," Brook said. In reality, she didn't have much faith in this method. Tom was an amateur, which was endearing, but when it came to this sort of thing, she liked to have more to go on than a tourist map and a hunch.

"Sometimes it's better to be lucky than good," Tom told her, sensing her skepticism.

"Right," Brook said without any conviction.

*   *   *

Professor Green couldn't understand it at all. Every other dog he'd ever heard of barked when the mail came and considered the postman a mortal enemy. Memphis, on the other hand, seemed to love the fellow, whimpering with delight on hearing his first approach and spinning in ecstasy until Green opened the door and let the animal bound out to leap up and lick the man's hands and face.

"Hey, Memphis," the mailman reciprocated with a pet, well used to the routine by now. "Who's a good dog? You got a package today, Doc, special delivery from Jordan. I don't know that I've delivered something from Jordan in all my years. Here, you sign while I..."

The postman juggled the package and electronic signature tablet while he squatted to trade affection with the dog. Green signed for his package and thanked the mailman, then brought the mail and a reluctant Memphis back inside his apartment.

Careful to preserve the section containing the return address in Amman, he opened the large, padded envelope, and recognized the book right away as the one Brook had sent scans of through email. He ran his fingers over the two-headed eagle on the cover.

"The Royal Seal," he whispered. As old as he was, and as many things as he'd seen, he wasn't past being awed by a truly rare artifact. He wouldn't touch the seal again, not without gloves.

Carefully, Green placed the book down. He found a note in the envelope:

G —

Changed mind. Safest with you. See what you can find out, please! On the Q-T.

BB

He stared at the note. It was written on the back of a sheet of crumpled-up paper with Arabic printing on the other side, as though Brook had fished it out of trashcan on the street. The envelope was new, and hastily addressed in the same handwriting. There was a feel of desperation about it all, Green sensed. He carefully folded up the note, put it aside, and picked up the book again, then sat down and opened it to the first page; blank. As he turned it over in his hands, he noted that the binding was intact.

"Hold on, what's this?" he muttered. The inside cover was thickly padded, as though the wood or pasteboard had swollen from moisture, but the back binding seemed unaffected.

Green toyed with a raised shred of paper in the corner. To his surprise, it took little coaxing to pull the paper further and reveal something hidden under the page—more paper. Green worked the sheet out, careful not to damage it. It was a thin, folded parchment that looked as if it had been traced from another document—comprised of dots and lines like a connect-the-dots game you'd find in a child's magazine or a star maps, like the one used to identify the location of Cleopatra's tomb.

"Well, well, what do we have here?" Green stated archly in his thickest cockney.

He took out his phone and dialed. "Nestor? Remember that book? The one in Greek, with the Tsar's seal."

He paused, listening.

"It was just a guess, I understand—you wouldn't bet the farm on it. Anyway, I've got it."

Another pause.

"Right, in my hot little hands. Can I bring it to you?"

Green waited.

"That would be good. I don't drive at night so well anymore. See you soon."

Nestor had offered to put Green up in his spare room overnight—it was a five-hour drive.

"Come on, Memphis, we're going on a road-trip to see Uncle Nestor."

The dog wagged his tail, trusting that whatever his master was talking about would be fun.

* * *

Fortunately, the Moscow River was low. There'd been a drought through the summer, which meant the water between the two bridges was only a ten-foot wide stream.

"You know what I think?" Tom said as he and Brook walked the narrow walkway above the river—the route was likely forbidden, but there was no easy access to the embankments below.

"No, actually, what do you think?" Brook asked, genuinely interested.

"I think you should write your book."

"Like you did?"

"I had to. I was compelled," Tom replied, "but I didn't want to. I wanted *you* to. Nobody wants to read my book—"

"It's a best-seller!"

"Second choice, that's all," Tom protested. "People want to read *your* book. *I* want to read your book."

"That's very kind of you." She stopped and looked over the vastness of the river. "So, what are we looking for?"

"A door," he replied, grinning at the ridiculousness of it. "A big oak door with a padlock and a sign that says 'Library.'"

Brook laughed, and squatted to the floor. "This wasn't always paved," she said, waving her hand across the expanse.

"Maybe there are pictures. It's a real long shot, but mining operations find all sorts of things under the ground..." Tom suggested, thinking out loud.

"Can you imagine what kind of juice it would take to do underground radar scans here?" Brook asked rhetorically, looking out at the huge, imposing buildings of the Kremlin.

"Strelov could do it."

"I'm sure he thought of it," Brook said, "but that's not the way he works. He's not a 'plays well with others' guy. The loot would belong to *them*," she pointed at the Kremlin, "not Strelov."

"He thinks you have a map to a secret entrance?"

"Apparently," Brook shrugged.

"Do you?".

She laughed.

"So you don't trust me, either?" she said with a smile.

"Just asking..."

"I don't *think* I do, and even if I did, I'm not sure I want to dance with that devil, no matter how much I like the tune."

"And what tune it that?" Tom asked.

"Putting the past right, getting justice."

"Justice for who? Your father?"

Brook thought about that for a moment.

"Actually, I was thinking bigger," she said, "but yeah, for him, too. Strelov is willing to trade me something that would go a long way to reinstating the reputation of Cale Burlington. All I have to come up with is a way into the hidden basement of *that,* "Brook said, pointing again at the massive fortress across the river.

27

Negev, Israel, 1948

Lev Abramovich was used to discomfort. In fact, his whole adult life had been marred by discomfort, and before that, most of his life as a child in Moscow.

But this itch!

His uniform was scratchy in the Negev heat, very scratchy. He lay prone in the sand, submachine gun aimed southwest, ready for the Egyptians, who were close, everyone said. The settlement of Kfar Darom that he and his fellow Haganah had pledged to defend was at his back. Beyond stood the new State of Israel, declared independent one day earlier, on May 14, 1948.

It was the second country Lev had been privileged enough to be present in at its birth, he noted with pride, remembering the Independence Day he had witnessed in Transjordan almost exactly two years earlier.

"The day you sold the book," Lev muttered to himself bitterly.

"Shut up!" the soldier to Lev's left hissed.

Lev didn't answer, knowing the other man was right. Any disruption of the peace would almost certainly give away their cover, and so they sat in silence, buried in the sand, a secret army of ants ready to jump up and surprise the Egyptians.

His arrival in pre-independence Israel hadn't ended all of Lev's misery. He shook his head, trying to erase the two years of memory that lay in his surroundings—scrounging for work explaining himself over and over, spinning one lie after another, never getting close to anyone, and always on the move within Jerusalem; on the coast, in the mountains, wherever he could find shelter and a crust of bread.

But it turned out okay, he assured himself. He had joined the Haganah more out of necessity than conviction, though the organization's steadiness and camaraderie had helped him immensely. In particular, it had given him hope again; enough to allow his plan for the future to evolve. While lying in the sand that day, he had already reviewed it many times to ignore the heat and discomfort. First, he was to secure citizenship—officially, he wasn't recognized as anything; not Polish, nor Russian, nor Israeli yet, and he was tired of it. Second, he had to get a passport with it, and third, go back to Moscow. Nobody would recognize him there now, he was certain. All his old friends were gone, and his family was no doubt scattered to the wind, if any had survived. He knew how to get back to the library, and the vast riches there. He didn't need a map; he'd memorized it long ago, and remembered that night like it was yesterday. He would go back underground, take as many of those books he could carry, night after night until they were all gone, and sell them for top dollar—no haggling. They owed him that, Lev figured, after what they'd done to him and how they'd destroyed his life these last twenty years.

The next part of the plan wasn't as clear. With millions—whether dollars, rubles or pounds, Lev wasn't sure--he could live whatever lifestyle he wanted with whatever time he had left. He knew it wouldn't be in any country he'd been to yet; the urge to see the world still called. Perhaps America, Italy, England, or France—somewhere he could be alone if he wanted, or with people, if he ever learned how. He'd choose a villa possibly, near a large city. He'd have a driver—

The rumble of the tanks snapped his focus back to the present; it was the first signal. There were hundreds of them, followed by other vehicles as well. Egyptian soldiers in trucks jumped to the ground, swinging their rifles, but not firing yet.

Lev tensed, resisting the urge to pull the trigger and send death and destruction into their ranks.

Wait, he'd been trained. Make every shot count.

A few bursts of light were all he saw from the rifles of the opposing force before a bullet found its mark through his eye and bored deep into his skull, ending Lev Abramovich's life, his misery, and his dreams, instantly.

28

Ocean City, MD / Moscow

The Professor Green couldn't understand it at all. Every other dog he'd ever heard of barked when the mail came and considered the postman a mortal enemy. Memphis, on the other hand, seemed to love the fellow, whimpering with delight on hearing his first approach and spinning in ecstasy until Green opened the door and let the animal bound out to leap up and lick the man's hands and face.

"Hey, Memphis," the mailman reciprocated with a pet, well used to the routine by now. "Who's a good dog? You got a package today, Doc, special delivery from Jordan. I don't know that I've delivered something from Jordan in all my years. Here, you sign while I..."

The postman juggled the package and electronic signature tablet while he squatted to trade affection with the dog. Green signed for his package and thanked the mailman, then brought the mail and a reluctant Memphis back inside his apartment.

Careful to preserve the section containing the return address in Amman, he opened the large, padded envelope, and recognized the book right away as the one Brook had sent scans of through email. He ran his fingers over the two-headed eagle on the cover.

"The Royal Seal," he whispered. As old as he was, and as many things as he'd seen, he wasn't past being awed by a truly rare artifact. He wouldn't touch the seal again, not without gloves.

Carefully, Green placed the book down. He found a note in the envelope:

G —

Changed mind. Safest with you. See what you can find out, please! On the Q-T.

BB

He stared at the note. It was written on the back of a sheet of crumpled-up paper with Arabic printing on the other side, as though Brook had fished it out of trashcan on the street. The envelope was new, and hastily addressed in the same handwriting. There was a feel of desperation about it all, Green sensed. He carefully folded up the note, put it aside, and picked up the book again, then sat down and opened it to the first page; blank. As he turned it over in his hands, he noted that the binding was intact.

"Hold on, what's this?" he muttered. The inside cover was thickly padded, as though the wood or pasteboard had swollen from moisture, but the back binding seemed unaffected.

Green toyed with a raised shred of paper in the corner. To his surprise, it took little coaxing to pull the paper further and reveal something hidden under the page—more paper. Green worked the sheet out, careful not to damage it. It was a thin, folded parchment that looked as if it had been traced from another document—comprised of dots and lines like a connect-the-dots game you'd find in a child's magazine or a star maps, like the one used to identify the location of Cleopatra's tomb.

"Well, well, what do we have here?" Green stated archly in his thickest cockney.

He took out his phone and dialed. "Nestor? Remember that book? The one in Greek, with the Tsar's seal."

He paused, listening.

"It was just a guess, I understand—you wouldn't bet the farm on it. Anyway, I've got it."

Another pause.

"Right, in my hot little hands. Can I bring it to you?"

Green waited.

"That would be good. I don't drive at night so well anymore. See you soon."

Nestor had offered to put Green up in his spare room overnight—it was a five-hour drive.

"Come on, Memphis, we're going on a road-trip to see Uncle Nestor."

The dog wagged his tail, trusting that whatever his master was talking about would be fun.

*   *   *

Fortunately, the Moscow River was low. There'd been a drought through the summer, which meant the water between the two bridges was only a ten-foot wide stream.

"You know what I think?" Tom said as he and Brook walked the narrow walkway above the river—the route was likely forbidden, but there was no easy access to the embankments below.

"No, actually, what do you think?" Brook asked, genuinely interested.

"I think you should write your book."

"Like you did?"

"I had to. I was compelled," Tom replied, "but I didn't want to. I wanted *you* to. Nobody wants to read my book—"

"It's a best-seller!"

"Second choice, that's all," Tom protested. "People want to read *your* book. *I* want to read your book."

"That's very kind of you." She stopped and looked over the vastness of the river. "So, what are we looking for?"

"A door," he replied, grinning at the ridiculousness of it. "A big oak door with a padlock and a sign that says 'Library.'"

Brook laughed, and squatted to the floor. "This wasn't always paved," she said, waving her hand across the expanse.

"Maybe there are pictures. It's a real long shot, but mining operations find all sorts of things under the ground..." Tom suggested, thinking out loud.

"Can you imagine what kind of juice it would take to do underground radar scans here?" Brook asked rhetorically, looking out at the huge, imposing buildings of the Kremlin.

"Strelov could do it."

"I'm sure he thought of it," Brook said, "but that's not the way he works. He's not a 'plays well with others' guy. The loot would belong to *them*," she pointed at the Kremlin, "not Strelov."

"He thinks you have a map to a secret entrance?"

"Apparently," Brook shrugged.

"Do you?".

She laughed.

"So you don't trust me, either?" she said with a smile.

"Just asking..."

"I don't *think* I do, and even if I did, I'm not sure I want to dance with that devil, no matter how much I like the tune."

"And what tune it that?" Tom asked.

"Putting the past right, getting justice."

"Justice for who? Your father?"

Brook thought about that for a moment.

"Actually, I was thinking bigger," she said, "but yeah, for him, too. Strelov is willing to trade me something that would go a long way to reinstating the reputation of Cale Burlington. All I have to come up with is a way into the hidden basement of *that,* "Brook said, pointing again at the massive fortress across the river.

29

Morgantown, WV / Moscow

Green arrived at Professor Nestor Petrykin's house in the early afternoon. Memphis leapt out of the car and loped over to his familiar friend almost before the door was open, and the man grinned widely. Petrykin loved the dog as much as the dog loved Petrykin. The big Russian put down his glass of beer, rubbed Memphis all over, and growled in his ear, sending the dog into a fevered run up and down the street at breakneck speed, which made both Petrykin and Green laugh out loud.

"Come in, come in, my friend," Petrykin insisted, grabbing Green's overnight bag from the car while Green retrieved the small package containing the book.

Petrykin's place was humble, clean, and a real academic's lair, with books lining every wall and the overflow neatly stacked in piles on the floor. It was built in the early 20th-century and of simple wood construction; nothing fancy, but not cheap or vulgar either.

"Welcome, welcome," Petrykin went on. "I will put your bag in the guest room."

"Thank you."

"You must have a beer after your long journey!" he called.

"That would be wonderful," Professor Green replied, collapsing into a chair while Memphis explored the rest of the house.

Nestor Petrykin and Green had been friends of his for the last ten years. Nestor had been a visiting professor at WVU originally, teaching Russian History. He had fallen in love with the United States, and begged the university to let him stay on.

While the US and the university believed it was a good idea, the Russian state wasn't convinced. Eventually, however, Petrykin was allowed to stay.

"It was a difficult period in Russian history," he was fond of saying, "but then what period *wasn't* difficult in Russian history?!" Then he'd laugh that big endearing laugh of his.

He and Professor Green bonded instantly. They were both bachelors—"troubled loners!" Green often declared to his friend— ex-pats, and hopelessly dedicated to their fields of study. Despite their enormous differences, they got along "famously," as Green would put it.

Petrykin returned with a glass of ice-cold beer for his old friend as Memphis collapsed on the floor.

"There is the book," Green said, pointing at the package he'd placed on the coffee table.

"Ah ha," Petrykin replied. "One moment."

Petrykin left the room again, and after a few seconds Green could hear him washing his hands in the kitchen sink. He returned a few seconds later drying his hands on a towel. In his pocket was a pair of latex gloves. Green smiled as Petrykin put them on. He too had a box of gloves ready and waiting in his kitchen.

Habit of the profession, he thought.

Petrykin took out the book and the sheet of folded up paper from the package.

"So, Stuart, this was hidden in the lining here?" Petrykin mimed the removal of the page from the book.

"Exactly."

"Okay, let me look at this book first."

Green watched the master go to work, inspecting the volume from every angle. It didn't take long before he reached a verdict.

"It looks to be from the correct period, certainly. Sixteenth century. And that's the Tsar's seal, I'm positive, unless it's a forgery..." Petrykin looked inside the book. "Greek. My Greek isn't what it should be—too much football when I should have been studying—but it's of the right period. The workmanship suggests a very expensive book, but not too fancy. To be read, rather than admired. Do you know what it says?"

Green shook his head. "Until today I only had a few photographed pages, which I sent to be translated."

"Constantin?" Petrykin asked.

"Yes, actually, but he never got back to me. I imagine he's busy."

"Not busy so much as troubled. The university is after him," Petrykin lamented.

"Really?"

Petrykin nodded gravely and made the universal gesture of tipping a bottle toward one's mouth.

"He sucks his thumb?" Green joked.

Petrykin faked a smile.

"Ha, ha," he said. "We should get him this book—no, a *copy*, he cannot be trusted at the moment. Is he the only Greek person we know in the whole world?" Petrykin wondered, annoyed.

"Could be," Green lamented.

"Okay, we will take the book to the copy place and copy some of it. If it's promising, we copy the rest. Now this..."

Petrykin unfolded the sheet of paper and carefully laid it out on the coffee table, careful to avoid Green's frosty glass of beer and any other contaminants.

"What is this?" the big Russian wondered aloud.

*   *   *

It had been Brook's idea to take the tour of the Kremlin; and Tom found it highly embarrassing. He'd lived in Moscow for two years, spoke Russian fluently, knew people who worked inside the building, and generally felt the plan was too 'touristy'.

"Have you ever actually *taken* the tour of the Kremlin?" Brook asked.

"Well, no," Tom admitted.

"See," Brook answered. "Locals never know what's right under their noses, do they?"

Having to admit it wasn't a *terrible* idea, Tom was forced to go along. Brook marched up to the gaudiest tourist kiosk on the square and purchased two tickets to the longest, most thorough walking tour, even when she was warned it spanned three hours total.

Inside, Brook shook her head as Tom headed to the back of the tour group, as if he could hide his big American frame that easily. More annoying was his insistence on augmenting the tour guide's explanations with knowledge of his own as if in competition to see who knew more about Russian history.

Brook was just about to ask him to relax—and "by the way, shut up"—when she felt her phone vibrate, reminding her she was in violation of the tour's strict 'no-phones, no cameras' policy. A surreptitious glance told her it was Professor Green calling.

* * *

"Mad, insane, crazy," was the only way Professor Green could describe the events of the day.

The craziness had started from the moment Nestor Petrykin opened the large sheet of paper that had been hidden in the book.

"I'm not sure what it is—" Green had started to say.

"Shh!" Petrykin had commanded.

He stared at the thing for several minutes while Green tried to sit perfectly still, not moving until his muscles began to cramp and he felt like he would explode.

"I know what this is," the Russian blurted, half-bragging, half groaning in frustration, "but I can't place it. It's a form I know well, I just can't..."

Green stood and examined the page with him.

"I was thinking some kind of architectural drawing?" Green suggested.

Petrykin shook his head violently.

"Or some kind of star-map?" Green tried again. "I helped Brook discover Cleopatra's tomb with the help of a star-map, you know—"

Petrykin gasped so sharply. Green worried the man was having a heart attack.

"Stop," he told Green, clutching his shoulder hard. "Don't move, don't breathe. I've got it! *You've* got it. A map!"

He jumped to his feet and ran around the living room like an insane man, grabbing a volume of the *Encyclopedia Britannica* and hurriedly locating Moscow. There were beautiful color photos, but they weren't what he was looking for. He checked the atlas. With a frustrated groan, he got up and ran back and forth around his house as Green watched, confused.

"I got it!" the man screamed from the back bedroom. There came the thunder of feet on the stairs, and Petrykin excitedly ran up beside Professor Green. In his hand was a book with a map of the area around the Kremlin. "See? What you have is rough map of the city of Moscow!"

He tilted the map slightly to match the angle of the much larger page.

"I don't know," Green hesitated, peering closer. Some of the lines were the same, certainly, and the dots maybe represented landmarks…

"This is it," Petrykin insisted. "Someone traced what you have from a large map, but they were either in a hurry or trying to be secretive, so never filled in the details."

"I'm still not sure."

"I'll show you. C'mon, let's go. Leave your dog," the Russian ordered as he grabbed his wallet and car keys.

"Where are we going?" Green asked.

"The copy store," Petrykin grinned.

"You want to enlarge the map in the book?" Green realised.

"Exactly."

"Why don't we find a map on the Internet and enlarge that?" Green suggested. He was wary of handing it over to a stranger.

"No internet here," Petrykin answered, as if the idea was outrageous. "I won't have it in my home."

"Then your office?"

"Spies," Petrykin whispered, waving away the idea. "It's the Russian Department!"

"Oh," Green replied simply, worried at the depth of Petrykin's paranoia.

"C'mon," the Russian urged. "The copy store will be fun!"

Green wouldn't have called it "fun", exactly but the experience was painless enough. In all his time at the school, he'd never been here, but now he found himself wondering if his students had, and for what purposes.

To Green's surprise, among Petrykin's many abilities was an apparent eye for enlarging maps. A couple of stabs followed by a small adjustment meant they quickly had an exact replica of the illustration Green had pulled from the book. In a final theatrical touch, Petrykin placed Green's page over the enlarged map so the lines and dots matched perfectly. The paper could have been a tracing of this very map.

"There's the Kremlin," Professor Petrykin hissed intensely, "and here is the river. And here," he said, catching his breath and choking a little, "here, at this little 'x' mark on the bank of the Moscow River, the only 'x' on this large sheet of paper, is the entrance to the Golden Library, the Lost Library of the Tsars, *Die Bibliothek des Zares von Moskau.*"

Professor Green jumped with surprise at his words—he'd purposely avoided mentioning the Lost Library.

"No, I'm not psychic," Petrykin told his old friend, "and you didn't 'spill the beans', as the Americans would say. You didn't need to say anything; I saw it in your eyes."

Green suddenly felt shaky and nauseous. He wanted to sit down, but there was no place to, so he tried to focus on something besides his own body. He checked his watch. It was ten p.m.

How long have we been in this God-forsaken place?

"What time is it in Moscow?" Green asked Petrykin urgently.

"Around noon," he answered without hesitation or looking at his own watch. It puzzled and surprised Green. Was Petrykin so attached to his homeland that he lived in its time zone? Or was he one of those *savants* who just knew, like somebody who could tell you what day of the week a certain date was in all of history.

"Noon, perfect," Green replied simply, pulling out his phone. He would worry about his friend's talents later.

*　　*　　*

The tour-guide was more than peeved when Brook had indicated she needed to use the ladies' room. The tour could not go on without her, the guide noted, and there would soon be a break near the gift shop. Brook apologized, but demanded to be shown the nearest facilities. Once inside, she dialed Professor Green's number. She'd ignored his first call, and hadn't listened to the message he'd left either, but when he texted "call urgently", she'd taken action.

"I've got something for you," Green announced as he picked up, obviously excited. "I need to send you a photo right away."

"Okay, do it," Brook answered, "but I can't talk now."

"Call me when you can?"

"Five minutes?"

"Got it," Green said.

Brook shut her phone off completely, flushed one of the toilets, and hurried out to the group, who all waited patiently, except for the tour guide.

"I'm feeling sick," she said. "I need to get out of here. I wouldn't want to throw up on all this priceless history—"

Tom, catching on though not believing the act one bit, held her gallantly as though prepared to carry her out.

"Wait!" the guide ordered. "You need to be escorted."

She barked irritably on her two-way radio, summoning security to escort Brook and Tom out. Brook couldn't blame them for their caution—if she was going to steal a state secret or a priceless piece of art or two, a fake illness would be the obvious first step.

Once out on the street, Brook called Professor Green.

"Did you get the map?" he asked.

"Is that what it is?"

"Yes, a map of the Kremlin."

"Oh..." Brook looked around, comparing the image on the phone screen to her surroundings. "We're actually there right now."

"The two strong vertical lines are the bridges on the south side that go across the river..."

"I can see them!" Brook realized. "They're very small on my phone, though."

"Can you see the 'x' mark?"

Brook squinted.

"Not really."

"It doesn't matter; I'm going to tell you where it is," Green assured her. "We've measured it and figured it out. Can you write this down?"

Brook signaled for a pencil and paper, and Tom, ever the Boy Scout, was able to hand them over. He fished a crumpled sheet of notepaper and a pen from his pocket, and as he gave them to Brook, he moved in to eavesdrop over the noise of the traffic.

"The total distance between the two bridges is about 3000 feet, or three-fifths of a mile," Green said.

"A kilometer," Tom interjected, writing the distance down.

"That's right," Green agreed. "Is that you, Tom?"

"It's me."

"Hello! Let me go on while I have it in my mind. The 'x' is about twelve hundred feet east of the westernmost bridge. In other words, you need to go to it and walk two-fifths of the way to the east bridge. The spot is there, on the Kremlin side. At that spot, there should be a door directly to the library."

Tom and Brook looked at each other. They had seen no doors. Maybe under all that concrete...

"Thank you, Professor," Brook said sincerely. "We have some work to do."

Green chuckled at the other end of the line. He felt tired and giddy, the way he had at the end of the Cleopatra adventure.

"Okay, then, cheerio," he said, signing off before scoffing at himself. He hated the expression. It belonged to a class of people he had left long ago.

*   *   *

It wasn't quite as easy as the professor had made it sound. For one thing, there was no access into the paved river chasm. Jumping a fence—even if it was possible—would likely get them arrested, and to add to the difficulty, the visibility into the river wasn't great on the Kremlin side.

"Okay, first step," Tom decided, "find the spot."

Tom marched off to the western-most bridge and started walking east, counting his steps. Brook walked along with him, not quite sure what he was doing.

"1457 steps," Tom announced when they'd reached the other bridge. "Now what's two-fifths of that?" He took a seat on the sidewalk, pulled out the calculator app on his phone, and started to calculate. "583, give or take. So we go back and mark off 583 from the other bridge."

"Could I make a suggestion?" Brook asked.

"What?"

"Subtract 583 from 1457, and we'll count off going back the other way. It'll save us steps. We just walked more than half a mile, and we'll be walking a half-mile back."

"Good thinking," Tom said. He got out his phone again. "874."

He jumped up, and they started walking back the way they came. When they found the spot, Tom tied a handkerchief to the guardrail to mark it. They locked hands, walked across the bridge, and checked the placement.

"You're the only man I know who still carries a handkerchief with him everywhere," Brook observed on the way.

"Well, that would be my father," Tom replied. "He insisted on it. Said it was the mark of a gentleman."

"Good for him," Brook said.

On the other side of the river, they looked back at the handkerchief flapping in the breeze. Below it, there was no sign of a door, just flat, smooth, gray cement.

"There it is," Brook commented. "Now that we know..."

"What are we going to do, come back here with a couple of jackhammers and start pounding away?" Tom asked.

"Why not?" Brook realized with great excitement. "Who asks a jackhammer operator what he's doing? You put up a bunch of orange cones, and people stay away on account of the noise and go on about their own business."

Tom chuckled and shook his head. "I hope you're not serious."

"It's not like we're going to wake anybody up," Brook added. "Listen."

She was right about that. The traffic going both ways along the river created a horrible din.

"Have you ever even operated a jackhammer?" Tom challenged.

"No, have you?"

"No, but I bet you need to know what you're doing," he reasoned, "and where to rent one."

"We hire a crew, that's all."

Tom laughed.

"Even the most hard-up day-laborer is going to balk at destroying the riverbank within sight of the Kremlin, and look at us. We're not exactly citizens of this country, either, it'd hardly reassure people."

"Wimp," Brook teased.

"Careful," Tom warned.

She took his arm, squeezing it apologetically.

"Let's go back. I have another idea," she said.

As they started to cross the bridge to the Kremlin again, Brook's phone rang. The caller ID wasn't familiar, but she answered anyway.

"Brook, it's Pejna."

"Good to hear from you."

"Can you talk?" she asked urgently.

"I...I don't really know," Brook answered honestly, making a U-turn away from the Kremlin, one of the most likely places in the world for a listening device to be located. Tom, puzzled, followed. Brook picked a spot where the cars made the most noise and the sound bounced off of the cement below before speaking again. "It's so loud here, I think it's safe."

"The Turkish National Intelligence Organization is on your tail, Brook."

"I think you're right. They searched my room in Amman."

"They did?" Pejna asked, surprised.

"Yes, it was ordered by a gentleman by the name of Mehmet Davidoglu," Brook answered.

Pejna gasped.

"Are you sure?" she asked.

"He gave us his card."

"Mehmet Davidoglu is the number one persecutor of the Kurds. He's very dangerous."

"I'm sure he is," Brook answered, "but there's not much I can do except run, which we did."

"Where?"

Brook wondered if she should answer, but decided to be honest; she had been forced to deceive her friend enough.

"I'm in Moscow," Brook told her, "near the Kremlin, actually."

"I will be there," Pejna replied without hesitation. "I will call you when I arrive and bring men with me who can fix this."

"Pejna, I don't really want to be involved in starting World War Three this week—"

But Pejna had already hung up.

"Who was that?" Tom, who had waited a little further back, wanted to know.

"Kurdish National Front asking for a donation," Brook joked.

"What were we doing?"

"You had an idea..."

"Right. Yes, I did. Let's go."

They started across the bridge toward the Kremlin again. As they walked, it started to rain hard, one of those sudden storms which could even grind a city as large as Moscow to a halt in seconds. Brook and Tom ran, finding shelter under a large tree.

"If it starts to thunder and we spot lightning, this probably isn't the best place to be," Tom pointed out.

"At the first sign, we'll run," Brook agreed, "if we're not burnt to a crisp first, that is."

"What was your idea?" Tom asked.

"It's nothing genius," she said, "but let's see if there's a softer point of entry into the tunnel we think is straight down from our marked spot." Brook pointed to Tom's handkerchief, which still blew in the breeze.

"A line from there to the library under the Kremlin?" Tom said, catching on. He drew a line in the air with his finger, but quickly realised the idea was too broad. "It's a big building—well, complex of buildings, really. The tunnel could go anywhere along this block."

Brook, her shoes filling with water from the rain, took a frustrated step away from the tree. Tom, too, had to move—for some reason, the flood headed right for them, into a drain.

Tom looked down at his feet and gasped with surprise, prompting Brook to hurry over. There was no grate—this was some sort of void, perhaps an underground spring, or—

"Sometimes it's better to be lucky than good," Tom said, grinning widely as realization hit.

"I'm really beginning to hate that expression," Brook responded.

"I'm going to pretend to tie my shoe," Tom whispered. He did just that, bending down to check the tiny stream that now flowed into the hole. He flicked on the flashlight on his phone and took a look, then stood up quickly. "Something there," he told Brook. "Definitely something there. It could be big enough for a real tunnel, or maybe it's part of the sewer system, but there's a chasm, about a six-foot drop."

"We should go and come back later," Brook said, conscious of how long they'd loitered.

"That way!" Tom said, grabbing her hand and running away, laughing.

Just like a couple of lovebirds on a nice vacation, the man under the umbrella who had been pretending to wait for the bus noticed. He walked away casually, and followed the pair at a safe distance.

30

Moscow

Mehmet Davidoglu thought about his family as he sat in the Moscow hotel lobby waiting for Tom and Brook to arrive. His wife and five daughters were what drove him— his weakness, he knew.

"A man attached to something can be easily manipulated," he'd been taught that lesson by some of the best persuaders in the world. He wondered what Brook and Tom were attached to. Each other, certainly, but that only went so far, from what he could tell. Perhaps their work?

Nobody dies for a piece of pottery, do they? he wondered.

There they are, he realized, spotting Tom and Brook coming through the front door, soaking wet. *So young...*

"Hello again," he greeted them, blocking their way to the elevator.

"Hello, Mr. Davidoglu," Brook answered.

"Ah, you remember!" Mehmet beamed flirtatiously. "It is a difficult name for a Westerner, I fear."

Not if you just heard it mentioned, Brook thought, but said nothing.

"Got somebody up there searching our rooms, do you?" Tom asked, acid dripping from his words as he took up a defensive stance.

"Alas, no," Mehmet complained, throwing his hands up. "No jurisdiction here. This is just a friendly meeting. Hopefully I can help you."

"How's that?" Brook asked, her voice equally as caustic as Tom's.

"I understand you are here to meet with a certain Russian oligarch?" Mehmet asked, eyes darting from Brook to Tom and back again.

Brook resisted the impulse to check Tom's reaction. He'd always been mysterious about his connections in this country. Perhaps Mehmet meant Strelov, perhaps someone else.

"I don't know what you're talking about," Tom replied guardedly.

Without looking at him, Brook couldn't tell if he was telling the truth.

Mehmet turned his attention to Brook.

"I know your friend Pejna has called you," he said.

Brook didn't say a word.

"And I know you met with your oligarch," Mehmet went on, directing his words to Tom now. "He has something she wants, am I right? Perhaps a certain signed treaty?"

Neither Brook nor Tom responded. He *was* talking about Strelov.

"Well, there is something you should know, both of you," Mehmet told them. "This billionaire is not the person you think he is. He wants to be richer than God. If this treaty is discovered, he'll make billions selling arms to the Turks and Kurds as they slaughter each other."

"And you think we can do something about that?" Tom challenged.

"I do, actually," Mehmet said, his tone easy like a friendly uncle. "Give me the treaty."

"We don't have the treaty," Brook admitted.

"Then get it for me."

"I don't think I want to do that."

He took a step towards her and leaned in, hissing into her ear. "Get me that treaty, or the world will find out that Brook Burlington is working for an international crime syndicate,"

"Now hold on—" Tom started to say.

Brook put her hand on his chest in a silent warning to stay cool.

"Just like her father," Mehmet added as he stepped away, placing his hat on his head. "People will believe it. What is your expression? 'The apple does not fall far from the tree?'"

Tom lunged to follow him, but Brook held him back.

"Don't bother. We have more important things to do."

31

"Who are we going to see again?" Brook asked. They were in a rental car, the sun was just going down, and Tom was driving too fast through the streets of Moscow.

"He's an old friend, Rastislav Derevev," Tom replied.

"Okay."

"He's going to help us."

"Is he a jackhammer operator?" Brook asked.

"No," Tom answered patiently, "but he's a good digger, with skills, equipment, and friends who are up for anything."

"So we *are* going down that hole!" Brook realized. She was suddenly so excited she could barely stand it. She'd been itching to dig since Libya.

"That's right...down the hole," Tom muttered hesitantly, suddenly worried this was a big mistake.

By the time they reached Rastislav's house it was fully dark. Rastislav himself was in a tiny one-car garage illuminated with a single overhead light, amassing rope, shovels, pickaxes, and flashlights.

"Tom!" he shouted gleefully as the rental car pulled up.

Brook watched the two men hug like long-separated twin brothers, slapping each other's backs and grunting greetings in Russian.

"And this must be the American sweetie," Rastislav proclaimed, grabbing Brook's hand and shaking it furiously.

"Brook," Brook said.

"Rastislav!" the Russian announced, beating his chest. "Would you like to come in for a drink?"

"We should probably get going," Tom suggested, raising a brow. He knew Rastislav would forget all about the matter at hand after a vodka or two.

"Yes, yes, the mission. Always the mission," Rastislav said glumly. He gestured to the pile of equipment behind him. "We put all this in the back of your little car."

"Where are the others?" Tom asked.

The Russian sighed.

"There are no others," he said. "I could not find anyone on such short notice. It is just me, but I'm a strong worker."

Rastislav hunched himself up and flexed like a body-builder, which made Brook laugh a little. Rastislav was turning out to be a colorful character, although she shouldn't have been surprised, knowing Tom.

"All right, then," Tom agreed, "just the three of us. Makes less of a scene, I guess."

They put the equipment in the back of the compact rental car. Tom and Brook got in the front as Rastislav shoehorned his large frame into the tiny backseat. After a few kilometers he noted a car behind them. "Don't look now, but we are being followed," Rastislav said as his head swiveled between their pursuer and Tom.

Tom checked, took a hard right turn at the next intersection, and then looked again.

"Three cars!" he said with a low whistle. "We must be something special."

Tom pumped the gas, and they flew through the still-wet streets of Moscow at top speed.

"They're keeping up," Rastislav commented.

"Okay, so we know speed won't lose them…" Tom announced, suddenly jerking the wheel to the left, skidding through the next intersection ahead of oncoming traffic.

The next vehicle behind did the same, but the second and third vehicles didn't make it. Oncoming cars smashed into them, knocking them up onto the sidewalk.

"Nice! One left," Rastislav called.

Tom considered, glancing at Brook.

"Just don't get us killed, please?" she begged.

Tom settled onto the wettest strip of road he could find, and slowed just a little, as if there were something wrong with the vehicle, thus allowing the sole car on his tail to catch up.

"Brace yourself back there," he warned.

Tom checked his own seatbelt, then Brook's. "You too," he told her.

Suddenly, he hit the brakes hard. The car skidded left, then right, and he fought against the wheel to keep control. The second they stopped, the pursuing car slammed into the back. Its hood popped up, and the sound of breaking glass and hissing steam filled the air.

Tom smashed the accelerator and took off, dragging the chaser's bumper with him for a few yards until it bounced to a stop. They all listened to the driver behind try and fail to restart their engine and continue the chase.

"You all right?" Tom asked Brook, concerned.

She rubbed her neck.

"Maybe a little whiplash," she managed after a few moments.

"I'm okay, too, you know," Rastislav said from the back, a smile in his voice.

Tom parked the car a couple of blocks from Ustyinky Square, and the three of them walked the rest of the way carrying their ropes, shovels, and pickaxes.

"If anyone asks," Rastislav said coolly, "we are doing a little gardening, that's all."

32

Moscow

The night was dark; there was no moon.

It continued to rain a little even after the deluge of the day, so there were no pedestrians to wonder what they were up to, and few cars driving by to ponder the same.

The opening proved easy to enlarge, and the tree next to it perfect for securing a rope around.

"I will stay up here," Rastislav announced. "To stand guard."

"You can't," Tom protested.

"Why not?"

"For one thing, you look incredibly suspicious standing here in the rain, and for another, we may need you once we get down there."

Rastislav shook his head.

"All my life," he said, "I have heard about what happens to people who get caught in tunnels."

Tom and Brook looked at each other and nodded, resigned. Neither really wanted to argue with the Russian.

"After you," Tom said to Brook, before hastily grabbing her arm. "No, wait—I'd better go first."

He stuck his flashlight between his teeth and rappelled his way down. As the rope slackened, Brook peered into the hole to see him standing in waist-high water ten feet from the surface.

"Come on in, the water's fine!" he announced.

Brook quickly followed.

They looked to the south, following the direction of the river, and could see the way was completely blocked by concrete. Neither said anything, but both knew that a sudden thunderstorm like the one earlier in the day would send them to their deaths against that wall; they would certainly drown.

The other way looked far more promising, with its rising gradient meaning that after a little way of walking, the water only came up to their knees.

The easy access ended abruptly, however, with dirt, mud, and debris blocking the way. In places, the tunnel was so constricted with silt, Tom and Brook had to crawl.

"Still think archeology is glamorous?" Brook asked.

"No, but I still love it," Tom replied.

They made it to a door guarded by two skeletons, made all the more eerie by the dull gleam of bone under the couple's flashlights. Brook took a picture with her phone. As the flash kicked in, she realized with horror that they weren't guards at all, but had been crucified in an apparent warning to any future trespassers, their hands and feet pinned to the wall by crude, rusty nails. She wasn't sure Tom noticed this, so she made no comment.

Tom seized the huge iron door, which was slightly ajar. He pulled with all his might, and the door creaked loudly enough to echo all the way back to the river.

Brook and Tom froze for a moment, certain they had been heard, but there was nothing more than the sound of only their own labored breathing.

The first glimpses of the library brought them both back to life. It was a huge, magnificent space, filled with shelves of books in their thousands. Many of the shelves had collapsed over the centuries, and haphazard piles of books were strewn everywhere.

"Nobody's been here in a long time, Tom," Brook whispered.

"I think you're right," Tom agreed.

She started taking pictures, then stopped abruptly.

"How should we approach this?" she wondered aloud.

"I don't know, you're the archeologist."

Brook shook her head. She noticed some chests, which were open a crack to reveal more books. These volumes were well preserved, she noted, unlike many of the books in the piles, which were damp, moldy, and many had been partially-eaten by insects.

"People have spent their entire lives looking for this library," Brook noted, "and yet we found it on the first try."

"Well, it's better to be lucky—"

"Don't say it. Please," Brook admonished, cutting Tom off

"Okay, I won't, but that doesn't make it any less true," he said. "Admittedly, it's not all luck. It's you; your talent for this. This is your *second* major discovery in less than two years."

Brook blushed, but waved the compliment away. She wasn't ready to open the champagne just yet.

"Like that one, this one was greatly influenced by Strelov," she pointed out, puzzling over the possible connection in her mind.

"I don't know..." Tom countered, but she held up a hand.

"It's time to break that chain," Brook vowed.

33

Moscow

"Yes?" Strelov answered the phone after only two rings.

"Mr. Strelov, this is Andre."

"Yes?"

"The man and woman have gone underground; into a tunnel, I think," the thug replied.

"Where?" Strelov asked urgently, leaning forward.

"The parkway south of the Kremlin," Andre told his boss. A second thug stood nearby, listening. They waited a hundred yards away, with a clear view both of the hole and of Rastislav sitting against the tree beside it, his face aglow with light from his cell phone. "They dug a hole with a pick and shovels."

"What?" Strelov asked, incredulous. "Right next to the Kremlin?"

"Crazy Americans, huh?" Andre commented.

There was a pause, and Andre began to sweat, sure he'd

overstepped his boundaries.

"Go get them," Strelov ordered. "Go down in the hole and get them."

"There's a man guarding it."

"Take care of him," Strelov said. "But don't kill him, he might know something. Tie him up and put him in the trunk of your car. We'll figure out what to do with him later."

"Then go down in the tunnel?" Andre asked, struggling to hide the fear in his voice. Ever since childhood, he'd had nightmares about going into a tunnel and not being able to find his way out. He had heard stories about what happened to people who were found in the tunnels.

"Yes, go down in the tunnel," Strelov ordered unsympathetically. He could hear the hesitation in the other man's voice, but didn't care. While Strelov could only imagine what might be contained within its four walls, he knew one thing for sure-- he *needed* to get in to that library.

* * *

Rastislav looked up from his phone and glanced around. He wondered if he'd genuinely heard something, or if it was just his imagination. His capacity to spook himself was enormous, he knew. He'd dodged the terror of the closed space below, but was guard duty really any safer? He was alone here. He looked at the pickaxe and shovel sitting on the ground, and the rope dangling into the hole. If the authorities came along, he didn't have a good explanation for the rope.

"Doing a little gardening," he muttered a couple of times as a rehearsal, trying to make it sound reasonable. "No," he chuckled. "I'm doing a little fishing...what, I'm doing it wrong? How stupid of me. No wonder I haven't caught any fish!"

He considered taking the tools back to the car for the sake of credibility. Maybe he could cover the hole with his jacket?

Rastislav weighed the pros and the cons—it would be cold without the jacket and it was a hike back to the car. Plus, what if Tom and Brook came up during that time and he wasn't there? What if they needed him and he had vanished? He wasn't sure their cell-phones worked down below anyway. What if someone came along— perhaps from the same gang who had chased them earlier—and there was no one to protect the hole?

The clunk on the back of Rastislav's head came suddenly, painfully, and without warning. As he fell to the ground, the Russian had the comforting feeling that whoever had delivered the blow hadn't meant to kill him, just knock him out. It hadn't been enough, and Rastislav suffered the pain. He moaned.

"Shut up," a voice hissed, and Rastislav felt some sort of cloth gag forced into his mouth—by the smell and taste, a filthy old sock.

He felt tape being pressed over his eyes and his arms being tied behind his back, and was then jerked to his feet and duck-walked off.

"Get the phone," he heard the man say to another in Russian.

The three of them headed out of the park area while a group of five other men watched the entire scene unfold from their hiding-place nearby.

34

Moscow

"What's that?" Brook whispered, her head jerking up from an interesting book she'd found in one of the cases.

"Footsteps!" Tom hissed back.

They turned off their flashlights and hid behind a pile of books. It wasn't a completely foolproof hideout; anyone with a flashlight who flashed a beam in their direction would easily spot them.

Tom drew a pistol from the back waistband of his pants, and Brook gasped as beams flickered over their heads. The footsteps had entered the chamber; now they were closer, there was clearly just one set. A single person, stopped on the other side of the room.

"Maybe it's your Russian friend..." Brook dared to whisper.

They heard the person turn swiftly at the sound, their sneakers scraping on concrete.

Tom jumped out, gun drawn, spotting the intruder—*not Rastislav!*

"Stop right there!" Tom announced. "Hands in the air!"

One hand rose slightly.

"I said, *hands in the air!*"

Tom fired one shot over the silhouette's head to show he meant business.

"I can't!" Pejna screamed in frustration from across the chamber. "I injured my good hand in the car crash. I was in the third car that was following you. I'm turning on my light now..."

By the light of Pejna's flashlight, held by Pejna's mangled hand, she looked pathetic. Blood flowed freely from her other hand, now totally useless.

"Brook?" Pejna called. "Are you there?"

Tom and Brook gave each other a look.

"Yes," Brook said finally. "What's this about? Why are you here?"

Before Pejna could explain, gunfire broke out right outside the library. They echoed deafeningly through the vast tunnels of cement surrounding the large room.

"We have to get out of here!" Brook screamed.

"I saw another door!" Pejna screamed back, pointing her flashlight to a spot on the wall seven feet up. Indeed, there was an outline of a large ornate oak door just visible above a fallen avalanche of books. Brook and Tom made their way in that direction, meeting up with Pejna on the way. Pejna and Brook embraced briefly.

"No time for that. C'mon!" Tom exhorted them, grabbing books and tossing them as far from the door as he could, three or four at a time. It was a monumental task, but the gunshots that continued outside the door gave them an almighty incentive.

"We need a bulldozer!" Tom complained. He put his shoulder to the pile and tried to push the books sideways, but it was too heavy. He went back to tossing aside several at a time—effective, but slow.

Outside, the gun battle died down.

"That's good news," Tom noted

They heard voices in Russian echo down the passage.

"My friends are dead!" Pejna lamented.

"How do you know?" Brook called.

"They don't speak Russian—"

"Look!" Tom interrupted. He'd just uncovered the large brass doorknob on the large oak door. "It pushes inward! We don't have to uncover the whole thing."

Tom turned the knob; it wasn't locked either. He pushed with all his might, but the door barely budged an inch. Pejna and Brook joined in, throwing their shoulders to the door, feet slipping over the books like sand at the beach. Brook kicked a few out of their path, noting the tradeoff—a whole room of priceless treasures damaged for a couple of lives. Men had died to save artifacts like these in Iraq, in Afghanistan, in Europe during both wars, and throughout the ages, no doubt. She thought back to Neferu, who'd risked his life to keep the remains of his beloved Cleopatra out of the hands of the Roman legions.

"And here we are running like scared rabbits!" Brook spat out loud, eliciting a puzzled look from Tom as the three of them pushed against the door, opening it a full two inches. For some reason, the Russians hadn't entered yet. Tom figured they heard his gunshot and weren't in any hurry to step into an ambush.

Realizing the door would never open that way, Tom desperately looked around for help. He spotted an iron pipe; six feet long and either part of the collapsed plumbing or the support structure for the walls of shelves.

"Stand back, ladies!" he announced in his best hero's voice.

He charged forward, pushed the pipe through the opening in the door, and began to push.

"Give me a lever..." Tom grunted, "and a place to stand..."

Brook and Pejna joined in pushing hard on the bar.

"And I shall move the world!" Tom and Brook roared in unison, calling on Archimedes' help as they wedged the door open just enough to escape.

They squeezed through seconds before they heard the Russians enter at the other side, guns blazing.

The next chamber was exactly like the first, so much so that Brook wondered exactly how many there were. Books and shelving blocked the door they'd just come through, but the pile was nothing like the mountain on the other side.

Tom shone his flashlight. The opposite wall held another exit, this one fairly free from debris.

Brook started to run to it.

"Wait!" he shouted, pushing hard against the door behind him in an attempt to close it again, but there was no key, no way to lock it. "Let's—"

Tom broke off as he started piling books against the door. Pejna and Brook joined in just as bullet holes from high-powered weapons blasted through the solid oak door.

"Get back!" Tom ordered, pulling out his pistol, but quickly realizing how useless it would be. "*Way* back!" he added, leaping high onto a nearby ceiling-bank of shelves, and leaning back with all his might, pulling the decrepit, worm-eaten mass right down on top of him before leaping to the side like a stunt-master on the set of some sort of big Hollywood action film.

With a final hoot from Tom and a deafening crash, the books and shelves covered the door. There was no way anyone would get through in less than a day without power tools and some serious muscle.

"Let's go!" Tom shouted, charging across the room to the other door, leaping over books and shelving like they were part of a hurdles race at the Olympics. "Sometimes it's better to be *good!*" he gloated.

*   *   *

Finally, Rastislav found the exact position to place his hands in. The trunk of the vehicle had been badly damaged by a rear-end crash—sustained that very night during the car chase, he guessed—but it had taken him a long time to find a sharp edge he could use to free himself. They'd only used duct tape, and despite the fact they'd gagged and bound him, even in the dark, airless confines of the trunk, it only took a minute to free his hands. As if on cue, his second phone rang in his pocket.

* * *

Brook, Tom, and Pejna soon came to a dead end. There was a manhole-cover type plate high above them; possibly a way out, but without a ladder, there was no way to reach it.

"Chances are it's locked anyway," Tom reasoned.

"Or goes right into a room in the Kremlin," Brook thought aloud.

"Or was cemented over a hundred years ago," Tom added. "The good news is, the immediate danger seems to have passed since I blocked that door, and we passed two other side passages getting here. Let's try those."

"You never answered my question," Brook said to Pejna as they started walking back the way they came. "What *are* you doing here?"

"The Turks were never going to let me live, so I was forced to become involved in the fight again," Pejna told her old friend. "They want the Kurdish treaty destroyed forever. I can't let that happen if I can help it. I don't know where you stand, Brook, but that's where I do."

Brook nodded, but did not answer. She stood with Archaeology...*but was that enough?*

35

Andre and his companion finally gave up on the door. They'd wasted too much time shooting into it, trying to take it off its hinges, pushing it.

"It weighs a ton!" Andre's partner had complained.

"You're a weakling!" Andre had declared.

As they made their way back, the pair of them argued as intensely as two men carrying automatic rifles could argue without it devolving into gunfire.

"We found the tunnel, didn't we?" the second thug reasoned at as they reached the spot under the hole. "That's what the boss wanted, right?"

Andre shrugged. It would have to do. At least the knotted rope was still there to climb to the surface with.

"I'll go first," Andre said. He had half a mind to pull the rope up after him and leave his partner to rot in the hole.

"Hello..." Mehmet Davidoglu whispered, greeting the Russian

thug as he crawled out of the hole. Before Andre had a chance to react, his weapon was taken, his mouth covered, and a seriously painful hold placed on his arm by Mehmet's fellow intelligence agents. The same surprise attack was successfully launched and completed on Andre's fellow companion as he emerged.

"Are they down there?" Mehmet asked in Russian—first Andre, who refused to say, then the other thug, who nodded.

"You weakling!" Andre spat, taking a swift slap across the face for the outburst.

"Who do you work for?" Mehmet asked, changing his approach, like any good interrogator would.

"Your Russian is terrible," Andre answered.

This time, Mehmet just laughed.

"You work for Strelov, I assume?" he asked.

Andre said nothing.

"Scream if that's true." Mehmet said, stomping down hard on the arch of Andre's foot while elbowing him in the gut.

Andre let out a sound more like a groan than a scream, but it was good enough for his captor.

"I thought so," Mehmet said, giving the other thugs a quick wink. This show was for him. The more Andre resisted, the more the other one—who would certainly crack before long, Mehmet knew—would be persuaded by the agony he himself would avoid by cooperating.

In Mehmet's mind, the whole affair was a win-win situation.

Who's lucky now? Brook wondered as they walked down a long, narrow tunnel with no outlet. It ended in a concrete wall.

The second tunnel looked more promising, however, with another manhole cover that was complete with a row of iron footholds embedded into the wall. Tom climbed up first and tested their chances. It took quite a push, but the cover slid off, and Brook and Pejna felt cold night air rush in.

"Bingo!" Tom called gleefully. He climbed out, staying low, and looked around. He found himself in what looked like a place for Kremlin deliveries, with a one-truck loading dock. During the day, a car would probably have covered the manhole. "Come on up," Tom told the women. "Coast is clear."

Once out of the hole and safe in the shadows, Tom pulled out his phone and called Rastislav's number.

"Hello," Mehmet answered casually.

Recognizing the voice, Tom hung up immediately.

"Mehmet's got Rastislav's phone," Tom told the two women. "Let's hope he doesn't have Rastislav..." As he spoke, he dialed another number.

"Hey, Tom," Rastislav answered, just climbing out of the trunk of the car. He hurried quickly to a copse of trees for cover.

"You lose your phone?"

"They took it from me."

"Who?"

"A couple Russians. They locked me in the trunk of their car, but I freed myself and they don't seem to be around."

Tom hesitated. This could *definitely* be a trap of some kind.

"Are you still down in the hole?" Rastislav asked.

"No, we're up and out, but in a different location," Tom answered.

"I can see your car," Rastislav said. "I can get to it and pick you up."

"Do you still have the key?" Tom asked, kicking himself. If the Russian had been kidnapped—

There was a pause as Tom's friend searched his pockets and found the key, breathing a sigh of relief.

"I got it," he said. "They didn't search me."

Again, Tom became suspicious. Something wasn't right. If Russians had kidnapped Rastislav and not thought to search him, why did Mehmet have Rastislav's phone?

"Just tell me where you are," Rastislav said.

Tom had no intention of doing that, but even if he did, it occurred to him that he had no idea where they were.

"I'll call you back," he said hurriedly. "Don't call me."

Without waiting for an answer, he hung up.

"Okay, here's what we're going to do," he told Brook and Pejna. "We're going to figure out where we are and make our way back to the rental car on our own. Don't trust your eyes; they may have set a trap for us. I say we stay close to this building, move counterclockwise, and see if we can get our bearings."

Tom led the way, with Brook and Pejna following right behind.

"Would you put that gun away?" Brook whispered as they snuck around the building.

"I will not," Tom answered. "It's saved our lives once tonight."
He put his finger to his lips as they rounded the next corner.

There it was, their starting point—the tree, the hole in the ground, the rope, and the tools. But Rastislav wasn't there. Mehmet and his men were interrogating two Russians who looked familiar—*perhaps Strelov's men from the compound?* It was too dark to tell.

"Okay, we're going the other way," Tom whispered. They headed around the building in a clockwise direction. The presence of the men next to the hole was going to force them to take a long, circuitous route to the next bridge to the east. Tom figured that if they crossed and kept to the shadows, they could backtrack on the other side of the river and not be noticed. From there, they could cross the western bridge and come up on the rental car from the rear. If there was a trap, they'd have ample time and space to spot it before they were caught in it.

*   *   *

Mehmet Davidoglu had heard enough from the two Russians and his own men to know there was a gold mine just beneath his feet. He regretted that the two Russian thugs had killed the two strangers below in the process. Mehmet suspected the dead men were Kurdish fighters, and he would have liked to have captured them alive and interrogated them to discover how their presence fit into the puzzle.

Doesn't matter, Mehmet convinced himself. *I have what I need.*

He made the call.

"Strelov?" he asked.

"Who is this?" came the oligarch's reply in Russian.

"I'm here with a couple of friends of yours," Mehmet spoke casually in perfect English.

"I don't have any friends," Strelov replied. "Kill them."

Mehmet laughed.

"I like that, that's funny. You and me can make a deal, I believe. We have similar interests and we think alike."

"What do you want?"

"It's about what *you* want, Mr. Strelov," Mehmet said. "A certain library, maybe? There are mountains of books inside, I am told."

Mehmet held the phone up to Andre's partner, whose arm was twisted harder behind his back to force him to speak.

"Mountains of books," the man groaned in Russian.

Mehmet chuckled darkly as he came back on the phone. "So, are you interested?"

"How much? How much do you want?"

"I don't want a dollar, Mr. Strelov, or a ruble or a Euro. All I want is a certain document. The one you were willing to trade Miss Brook Burlington for exactly what I'm offering."

"Where is she?" Strelov asked.

"Out of the loop," Mehmet answered. "I am in possession of what you so greatly desire, not her. She can't help you now."

"Is she dead?"

"We're not killers, Mr. Strelov," Mehmet lied.

"Even if I say 'no?'" Strelov asked bluntly.

"'No' is not an acceptable answer," Mehmet replied. "So I *would* be forced to kill these men of yours—"

"Go ahead, kill them," Strelov answered coldly. "They are easily replaced."

"—and you, Strelov. You hear me?" Mehmet added angrily, switching to Russian for impact "And then I'll kill your family; every last member, you understand?"

"Take it easy," Strelov replied coolly in English. "We have a deal. I don't care about your ridiculous piece of paper. "He hung up slowly.

It would have been easier all around, he thought, *if they'd killed Brook Burlington when they had the chance...*

36

Moscow

As Tom, Brook, and Pejna made their way around the other side of the river to their rental car, many of the homeless who bordered it had settled into sleep, but others roamed the night, some smoking, some drinking, others either mentally unstable or high. Their presence proved to be both a blessing and a curse for the two Americans and one Kurd. On the one hand, they were harassed for money, cigarettes, and drugs the whole way along their path, but on the other, the movements of the trio did not stick out at all. Someone across the river—Mehmet and his men, for example, who they could clearly see—would easily have spotted them without the cover of others.

Rastislav did see them, however, and made his way to intercept them before they reached the rental car.

"Would you like a ride?" he asked casually once he reached them, holding up the key to the car.

Brook smiled gratefully and introduced Pejna before they all piled in. Rastislav insisted on driving, which made Tom's earlier suspicions flare again. He tried to protest, to keep control, but his argument was waved away.

"You get into too many crashes," Rastislav admonished. "Besides, I know the way."

"The way to where?" Tom asked, turning the blaring radio down, but not off. He couldn't be sure the car hadn't been bugged in their absence.

"My house, of course," Rastislav said. "You are all invited."

"Is it safe?" Tom asked cynically, scrutinizing his friend.

Is he against us?

Rastislav shrugged. "They never asked my name. They never took my wallet. They don't know who I am," he replied.

But Tom had stopped listening, and was leaning forward to turn the radio up again. An excited announcer could be heard rattling off breaking news.

Brook saw the simultaneous alarm on both men's faces as they listened.

"What is it?" she asked, poking her head between the two front seats.

"They're saying Kurdish terrorists are attacking in the streets of Moscow," Tom translated reluctantly.

Brook swallowed hard, and cast a worried glance over her shoulder. Pejna had gone pale.

"Supported by Americans, they're saying," Tom added.

"That's us," Brook realized with dread.

"Yeah, that's about right," Tom answered. He concentrated on the radio as Rastislav pulled over to the side of the road and turned the car's lights off, after which he listened too.

"'They are considered armed and dangerous'," Rastislav translated from the radio, "'and are suspected of stealing several priceless artifacts of national importance.'"

"You better not take us to your house," Pejna spoke hopelessly from the back seat. She suddenly looked frail and lost.

"She's right," Brook whispered.

"We can't go back to the hotel, either," Tom reasoned.

"You need to get out of the country," Pejna told them.

"*We* need to get out of the country," Brook corrected. "You're coming with us."

Pejna shook her head.

"I don't have my passport. I don't carry it. That way, if I get picked up, they can't connect me with my family or the network."

"Do you have your passport on you?" Tom whispered to Brook.

She nodded, "Do you?"

Tom nodded back.

"Where *is* your passport?" Brook asked, turning to Pejna.

Pejna thought about that, and hope glimmered in her eyes.

"It's at the safe house..." she said slowly, sitting up to lean toward Rastislav: "Drive again. I will direct you."

Pejna gave comprehensive directions from the back seat, steering the car through the dark streets of Moscow to a far end of town. With the damage to the rear, they soon found had they to go slowly. At a certain speed, the muffler bounced against the road and made a horrible racket. Any policeman within earshot would definitely stop them.

As they drove through street after street, it occurred to both Brook and Tom that Pejna might be taking them on a wild-goose chase; but for what reason, neither of them had any idea.

"How much further?" Brook asked gently.

"We're getting close," Pejna answered. "When we get there, we must go very carefully. We'll park a block over and make our way through the back alley. I will hurry in and get my passport. After that, we must separate. It would be ten times worse for you if you were caught with me. At worst, they will charge you and expel you from the country, but if you're with me they will press espionage charges. You could be sent to Siberia, or simply shot. They will probably shoot me," Pejna stated dimly. "After the torture."

After a few more miles, Pejna instructed Rastislav to pull the car over. They had stopped in a poor part of town on the outskirts of the city, a once-rural area comprised of shacks and makeshift tarp tents—a step up from the sewer dwellings of the homeless around the Kremlin, but only a small step. A freight train rumbled by, shaking the earth as a whistle pierced the night.

Tom started to get out of the car.

"No, please stay here," Pejna told him. Her tone was grave, and he did as she asked without protest. "When I have my passport, I will catch the next one of those trains going by. They slow here— there are many obstacles on the tracks; cows, goats, people, furniture. It's easy to get on. You go on; find the closest border and get across before they cast their nets. Goodbye."

Pejna started to get out, but Brook grabbed her arm hastily. She yelped—it was the wounded one.

"Sorry," Brook apologized, "but you're not going alone, and you're not going in some God-awful freight train. We're going to help you. There's got to be a better way."

Pejna choked on sudden tears. With her friends dead and her ordeal far from over, Brook's simple act was enough to send her over the edge of an emotional cliff. The two of them embraced and sobbed while Tom and Rastislav looked at each other helplessly.

Suddenly, Pejna could stand it no longer. She pushed Brook away, jumped out of the car, and ran a few yards down the road and into a narrow alleyway only a few feet wide. Brook jumped out with Tom right behind her, turning back at the last second to call to Rastislav.

"You stay here!"

Dogs barked, chickens clucked, and the tinny sound of radios and TV sets could be heard even in the middle of the night. The universal din of both live and recorded music filled the air; folk songs mixed with rap.

Brook was struck by the overwhelming smell of the place. Truly horrible odors intermingled with the delicious, exotic scents of ethnic cooking.

Pejna stopped at the back fence of a small house. A dim light shone inside. Brook and Tom came to a stop next to her as she contemplated her next move. Putting one finger to her lips, she sidled to the metal gate and silently opened it. Ducking low, she crept to the window from which the glow came. Brook and Tom followed suit, and the three of them rose in unison to peek over the windowsill.

An old TV was the source of the light. It was small, black and white, with rabbit ears that presumably picked up what little reception it could muster. To their dismay, it was set to the news, and photographs of Tom and Brook flashed on the screen; an odd combination of smiling publicity photos and dour driver's license and passport photos. They had pictures of Pejna, too—none of them smiling—as well as surveillance footage of Brook and Tom in various places around the Kremlin, though the quality of the images made identification impossible even when zoomed in.

Pejna turned her attention to whoever was watching. From her initial vantage point, all she could see were a pair of boots crossed on a vinyl-covered hassock. She angled her head to one side, and her view expanded to reveal dark trousers, then a uniform, a holster and side-arm and a standard-issue rifle—

A Moscow policeman!

As if on cue, a light blasted on, blinding all three of the voyeurs. Simultaneously, the frantic warning honk of the rental car could be heard in the distance.

"Freeze!" came the Russian shout from a bullhorn. "Hands in the air, don't move! We are the police! Make a move and you will be shot!"

Tom considered translating, but decided against it. Despite the language barrier, both Brook and Pejna knew what to do. They held their hands up and tried to stay still even as they shivered in fear.

37

Moscow

It had taken a month and the interjection of both the US and Jordanian embassies, but in the end Pejna was allowed to live, and merely deported back to Jordan, where she immediately disappeared into oblivion. The Turks had wanted her until the end, and even tried to bribe the Russians to release her to them, but she had finally been slipped quietly aboard a plane to Amman. Brook and Tom only hoped she hadn't been tortured once there.

"Pejna has suffered enough," Brook had said, before wondering aloud whether they had permanently cost her the use of her one good arm as well.

Brook and Tom had been jailed in Moscow on a number of charges, including looting and trafficking stolen antiquities, trespassing on government property, vandalism, the destruction of government property, reckless driving, hit-and-run, carrying an unregistered weapon, carrying a concealed weapon—you name it, they had been charged with it.

Brook's first call had been to her brother Carl, who had started the ball rolling on getting a private legal team together, as well as calling on the full weight of The United States of America via the State Department.

"It's going to take some time," he told Brook in one of the rare phone calls she was allowed.

"How long? When am I going to see a lawyer?" Brook asked.

The prison was maximum security; concrete walls and iron doors. The noise as they opened and closed was deafening. Brook was placed in a private five by seven foot cell in solitary confinement, allowed out only for a half-hour exercise period per day in a "yard" not much bigger than her cell, and was slowly deteriorating.

Alone, all Brook's demons—the ones who had been lurking in her head since the fateful incident at Woodburn Hall when she had seen her father wandering the hall—began returning. This time, there was no one to talk to, no one to call, and no drugs to "take the edge off". She was living on a razor blade, and the pain was excruciating, especially after it became clear the world would not be charging to her rescue. To quiet them, she played games in her mind—math games, word games, rattling off world capitals and listing every lyric to every Beatles song she knew. They gave her no books, nor paper or pencil to record what she was feeling, which made her even crazier. It was impossible to organize her panic in any way, and the sole guard with whom she had contact—a gray-haired woman she assumed was nearing retirement—would not say a word, not even in Russian.

Brook wondered if Tom was experiencing the same hell. In her most paranoid moments, she decided it was all designed to force her into suicide. So far she'd resisted, purely out of spite, though if they gave her a belt, a pencil—or anything sharp, really—she wasn't sure what she would do.

Brook wanted to convey all this to Carl during their phone calls, but there was never time.

"I won't lie to you, Brook," he told her eventually. "Everyone expects you to be found guilty. The best we can hope for is that they'll deport you, or do some sort of prisoner exchange."

"I understand," Brook told her brother. "I'm sure you'll do your best."

"I talked to Tom, and he seems to be equally resigned to his fate," Carl said. "He wanted me to tell you he loves you."

"Okay," Brook answered quietly. She didn't feel like sending love-letters through her brother right then.

*   *   *

The arrest of Brook Burlington swept across the international media landscape like a thunderstorm. Headlines accused her of being a real-life Carmen Sandiego, traipsing around the world and plundering priceless artifacts. Trying to steal something from the Kremlin was just one step too far. The news networks played up the "capers" of the so-called heist, repeatedly using file footage of the archaeologist in her skimpiest field outfits from earlier expeditions along with glamorous photographs of her dating back to her university days spent digging in exotic locales. She was an attractive woman, which made the story even more glamorous in a news cycle built on scandal and instant gratification.

Tom, too, was a prize subject. Young, handsome, rich, and the only one—besides Katy and her limited-release documentary—who had chronicled first-hand the discovery of the Lost Tomb of Cleopatra, he made for a terrific source of speculation.

The Bonnie and Clyde aspect of the whole affair fascinated everyone, and all sorts of interest suddenly became centered on the psychology of two seemingly young, attractive, well-respected people turning to a life of crime.

"Excitement junkies," some claimed of Brook and Tom, while other blamed an apparent death wish, or the fact that the pair were 'just nuts' for their actions.

The fact that they sat in separate prison cells in Russia and hadn't spoken a word to anyone-—let alone that no one knew exactly what they were accused of doing—didn't stop the stories, speculation, rumors, and lies.

Somewhat inevitably, the media grabbed onto the similarities with the Cale Burlington story. All the old allegations resurfaced—along with the news footage, interviews, and newspaper coverage—accusing him of "the biggest fraud in archaeological history".

Fortunately for Brook, in her Russian prison cell, she was blissfully unaware of her father's name being dragged through the mud again after all these years. Back home in Virginia, her brother Carl wasn't so fortunate.

38

Falls Church, VA / Moscow

They came in the morning, after Carl and the staff had just opened the doors to the Burlington Foundation. Their jackets said FBI, but there were others in plain clothes that outnumbered them. The warrant stated precisely what they were after; the canopic jar Brook had donated to the foundation's museum. The warrant claimed the artifact had, in fact, been stolen from the Iraqi government, and its rightful owner was the Baghdad Museum.

Carl was taken into custody, and the Burlington Foundation was placed under armed guard; left in the care of a couple of those plain clothes mystery-men who had bulges under their jackets. They awaited further orders, along with an army of forensics experts and accountants to examine the operation from head to toe.

Carl, fearful for the Foundation and desperately worried about the future for his wife and girls, tried to answer every question as accurately as he possibly could. He was well aware that misleading the authorities was a serious felony in itself.

"The jar came from my sister, Brook," Carl told them honestly. "She said it was an anonymous gift, and that's all she knew about it."

The FBI agents tried to dig deeper into the story, but Carl insisted that was everything he knew. Their questions turned to Cale Burlington and the numerous fraudulent activities he had been accused of during his lifetime, but they hit a brick wall there, too.

"I don't know anything about the accusations against my father. A lot of it was before I was born. I knew he'd had some trouble, but as his kids, we were protected. That has nothing to do with me." Carl had made this speech many times before.

Growing frustrated, they asked about the foundation itself.

"You track stolen artifacts from around the world, correct?"

"Yes..." Carl answered, sensing a trap. If they mentioned Redtail, he knew he was cooked—

"Like this jar, which was not only found in your possession, but which you had on display?" one agent accused.

"Brook brought it," Carl repeated. "She gave it to us, and we liked it so we put it on display. It's not stolen."

"Can you prove that?"

"No, of course not, but we check everything very closely," Carl insisted, finally showing a little indignation.

The agent who had asked the question tapped a ten-page document on the table in front of him. With the nodded agreement of the other, he pushed the papers to Carl.

He recognized the item right away—a standard stolen property report from Interpol, fully filled out with photographs, the date and time of the theft, and all leads afterwards, proven or speculated. He had seen thousands of them as part of his work at the foundation, and leafed through it quickly.

"This is a fake," he announced, pushing the item back across the table like it was contaminated.

"What makes you think that?" the FBI man asked, surprised.

"Because I would have seen it if it was real," Carl replied.

"That's all you're basing that on—you would have seen it, so for that reason it has to be a forgery?"

"That's right. A jar like that, I would have at least heard about. There would have been a heads-up phone-call as well," Carl declared.

"This came from Interpol." the FBI man said bluntly.

"If it really came from Interpol, it was slipped in after the date that's stamped on it," Carl insisted, getting testy. "We checked that jar—there was nothing filed on it at the time we accepted it, which was after that date. Somebody's trying to set me up—Brook and Tom, too."

"That would be Tom Manor, correct?" the FBI man said, flicking open his folder to check.

"Yes."

"Who is in a Russian prison awaiting trial for suspected grand theft from the Kremlin, among other things?"

"It's all a setup," Carl stated again.

"Uh-huh," the man said flatly. "Why?"

"I don't know why," Carl answered sincerely. "My guess is, my sister stuck her nose where it didn't belong...again." The minute he said the words, Carl felt guilty for. He wouldn't throw Brook under the bus no matter what, and reminded himself to stick to the facts rather than let long-standing family issues interfere with getting them all free from this mess.

"Where are the other two jars?" the other investigator wanted to know. "There are always four of these, right?"

"Yeah," Carl replied, "but I don't know."

* * *

"You have a visitor," Brook's guard told her one morning as she unlocked the cell door. They were the first words Brook had heard the woman speak in the three weeks she'd been incarcerated.

And in English, no less! Brook remarked to herself.

An aging Russian in a dark suit stepped into the cell and took a seat at the other end of her cot. He unfastened the snaps on his attaché case, but did not open it yet. Brook thought he looked like a lawyer of some kind, but he also seemed to be familiar with the tiny rooms of concrete prison housing. For a moment, she wondered if he wasn't there to assassinate her.

"Are you my lawyer?" she managed to choke out, backing to the far corner of the cell.

"No, I am not your lawyer," the man said. She detected a slight Russian accent.

The conversation changed to Russian. "May we be alone?" the man asked the guard, who had just locked them in.

"*Nyet.* You may not," the guard answered.

The lawyer—Brook was pretty sure now, despite his assurances otherwise—shook his head and finally opened his briefcase. Inside were a number of newspapers, magazines, and a portable DVD player. The man stood and spread the material out on the cot, then invited Brook to look at it.

The news of Brook's arrest seemed to have spread worldwide. Tom's featured heavily too, his face usually next to Brook's on the front page. Brook soon got the motivation behind all this—she and Tom were at the center of a worldwide scandal. Multiple news outlets reported the pair of them had planned and executed dozens of unnamed heists, apparently culminating in their arrest for a daring robbery of antiquities right under the nose of the Kremlin authorities. The media claimed they were certainly to be sentenced to life in prison, if not executed immediately for "crimes against the state".

An astute observer of human feeling, the lawyer quickly switched to the DVD when Brook's ability to digest the material before her flagged.

She saw news snippets that centered around her father, Cale Burlington, being accused of the same sorts of crimes, humiliated and broken. The phrase "the apple doesn't fall far from the tree" was repeated in a number of them.

Brook was far from broken, the man could see as he watched her increasingly incensed reactions. He fast-forwarded to Carl's arrest at the Burlington Foundation, a name the announcer was careful to spit out with a certain degree of derision.

Brook watched as the canopic jar was removed—seized as

stolen property, the report claimed— followed by the seizing of the complementary jar from a coat-closet in Tom Manor's high-rise New York apartment.

Brook was devastated. She'd ruined everything—for herself, Pejna, Tom, Carl, and Carl's wife and children.

She floated like a ghost over to the corner of the cell gasping like a drowning woman, and half-fell, half-slid to the hard cement floor. She sobbed and again thought fleetingly about hitting her head against the walls—*there are two here, it might just work*—

She stopped short as she felt the eyes of the man and the guard on her. She wouldn't give them the satisfaction.

"Okay, that's enough," Brook told the man. "Turn it off. Who are you? What do you want?"

Instead, the man turned the volume up a little on the continuous DVD. He came to Brook in the corner and slipped down to the floor with her, right next to the filthy, lidless toilet.

Whatever it is, this must be important, Brook decided.

*   *   *

The visit to Tom's cell was far less dramatic, and he understood what was on offer right away. Without the emotional baggage of family at risk, he was able to agree quickly. In exchange for not mentioning the library beneath the Kremlin to anyone for the rest of his life, a certain well-connected oligarch was willing to pay Brook and Tom's bail and use his influence to allow them to safely exit Russia. After that, at a time in the future when interest in the case had died down, this same wealthy individual would apparently see to it that all charges were dropped.

"What about Carl?" Tom asked. He had been shocked to recognize him on the DVD, and was all too aware of how much he meant to Brook

"Oh yes, Carl," the emissary was reminded. "That will be cleared up. It will be treated as an unfortunate misunderstanding on forfeiture of your canopic jar."

"And if I say 'no?'" Tom asked, stalling,

"If you say 'no,' Carl will be charged in the United States with possession of stolen property, as will you and Brook. The jars *are* stolen, and if necessary, the fact you stole them can be demonstrated beyond all reasonable doubt."

Tom stared at the man. Did he really have that much power?

"Of course, it would never get that far," the man said, in Russian now, "because if you say 'no' to one part of the deal, it's all off and you will never see the light of day. You will die right here in Russia, without a chance to tell your secret to anyone anyway."

"So what's the point of resisting?" Tom asked rhetorically.

"Exactly," the other man smiled.

Tom felt like giving the man a sock in the jaw, accompanied by a little speech about being honest with yourself and not caving in to thieves, bullies, or Russian oligarchs.

"Okay," Tom sighed. He responded in Russian, wanting to separate himself from the abandonment of all his morals. "I'll play ball. I don't care about your damn books. You can shove 'em up your—"

He stopped his monologue short as he noticed the indifferent expression of the man in front of him. There was no point.

39

Morgantown, WV

"'Disgraced Archeologist Returns to Campus'," Brook spat bitterly as she mixed herself a second cocktail while Tom tried to make supper in her Morgantown kitchen. Tom had never been much of a cook; a fact he was now demonstrating nightly.

"It couldn't have been as bad as all that," Tom tried gently.

"Oh, it was bad," Brook told him. She'd gone back to campus to retrieve her things, and had been mobbed by a swarm of people. Students, faculty, and even the janitor had given her the skunk-eye. In their eyes, she had worked for the Russian mob and tarnished their reputation—they'd seen it on TV.

"You know the university did it in stages, right?"

"What are you talking about?" Tom asked, putting their plates down on the dining room table.

"First they dropped me down from 'Distinguished Professor' to plain old 'Professor', then they took that away, too, tenure be damned—"

"Brook..." Tom sighed. He'd become weary of her self-loathing and the constant exaggeration of her misery. This wasn't the gutsy Brook Burlington he'd once loved, who laughed at every catastrophe.

Brook sensed Tom's impatience, which made her even angrier.

"They took the 'prestigious' Amelia B. Edwards Chair away, too, you know."

"I know," Tom said. "Could we just eat?"

They ate in silence, as they had many times over the past few weeks; until Brook began to cry, then sob. She got up from the table and hurried back to her bedroom, where Tom heard her collapse on the bed. He knew from experience not to go to her—it only turned her sorrow into fury, which prolonged the misery from a few minutes to days. He ate slowly, hoping she would come back to the table before he finished, which she did.

"I was thinking about Pejna," Brook explained as she sat back down.

"Oh," Tom replied, waiting for more.

"I hope she's all right."

"I hope so, too."

"I wish we'd found that document," Brook sighed.

Tom shrugged.

"I do too," he said, "sort of. But I don't think it would have done much good if we had."

"It established Kurdistan," Brook argued.

"On paper, maybe, but they'd still be fighting about it; it could have brought on even more fighting. More people could have been killed if the world knew."

Brook shrugged.

"You could be right," she said dejectedly.

For the past few weeks, they'd watched the news for information about the Kurds, searching for some glimmer of hope—some indication that the document they'd so eagerly sought had made a difference somehow. But nothing changed, only more news of the endless, useless conflict and stalemate.

"There are just places in the world that are always at war, and that's one of them," Tom concluded. It didn't look like Brook was going to start crying again, so he added. "They've been fighting our whole lifetimes, and our parents' lifetimes before that, and I'm sure they'll be fighting through our children's lives—"

"We aren't going to have children!" Brook spat angrily.

Tom was taken aback by the vehemence. It wasn't something they'd discussed.

"I'm done," Brook said, pushing her plate away. She'd eaten more than usual—that was a good sign. "It was very good. Delicious."

Tom smiled weakly; he knew better. Brook didn't respond except to leave the table and return to her room.

Later that night, Tom approached the bedroom carefully so as not to wake Brook, only to find her sitting up in bed reading a copy of his book. He knew she'd already read it, and had no idea why she'd read it again.

After all, she was there.

Sensing him at the door, Brook put the book down, made room for him, and nestled under the covers.

Tom undressed and joined her.

"The H stands for Hiram," he whispered in her ear. "My middle name...Hiram."

Brook didn't laugh the way Tom hoped she would, but she smiled in appreciation of the effort.

"I wonder how long it will take Strelov to mine the Tsar's library," she mused, sounding a little less bitter than she had at supper.

"Those two rooms alone will take a year if they don't want anyone to notice, and they won't," Tom answered.

"I wonder how many rooms there are," Brook reflected.

"We might not ever know," Tom answered. "But I'll tell you one thing; it's a good thing the books are in Strelov's hands, no matter how bad a person he is. They'll be taken care of, and eventually the world will harvest the knowledge contained in them one way or another. At least they won't be thrown on a bonfire somewhere."

"Like the Kurdistan treaty," Brook remarked.

"Well, you're probably right about that," Tom sighed. "The Turks probably did burn the thing at the first opportunity."

Brook rolled over and turned off the light, and that was the last time they ever discussed it.

Early the next morning, the house phone rang in the living room.

"Hello?" Tom answered.

"Hello, Tom," Professor Green said. "How is she?"

Tom was about to answer when Brook entered.

"We're fine," Tom hedged. "She's right here." He covered the receiver and gave it to Brook. "Professor Green," he whispered.

Tom took Saqqara out to the backyard and let the two professors talk alone. Green had insisted on trying to find Brook a position at another university. His network of contacts was "vast, simply breathtaking", he had announced with the sort of overplayed optimism Brook and Tom were grateful for, but knew was unrealistic.

"I'm so sorry," Green said into the phone that morning. "I have to be brutally honest with you, and it breaks my soul in two to say it, but in the eyes of the academic world, you're finished."

"Thanks for trying," Brook managed to get out, "and thank you for being honest with me." She hung up quickly and collapsed into the couch. Tom, who was listening intently outside, ran in with Saqqara to console her.

* * *

A month later, The Burlington Foundation closed its doors for good. Its government contracts had all been rescinded, and its reputation was in tatters, though the full extent of Redtail was never revealed. The media attention had nearly destroyed Carl, and there were rumors of marital troubles, though Brook had no way of knowing whether they were true—he had cut off all communication with her by then, hoping to "move on".

Brook's mother didn't want her to visit, either, which was okay by Brook. It would have only reminded her of the attic, her disgraced father, and the shotgun that had started the whole ugly affair.

Brook's old friend Katy had come to visit a few times. The Cleopatra film had turned out to be a huge sensation, released theatrically all over the world. Brook's downfall had multiplied interest tenfold, according to some analysts.

But when she was there, the closeness between Katy and Brook seemed to be gone, as if their adventures in Egypt and Libya had never happened.

Tom tried to get some sort of advice from Katy, but she only repeated his thoughts.

"Brook needs psychiatric help. She needs therapy. Maybe medication. She's depressed."

Tom sighed at that. He had tried, but without Brook's cooperation, there was nothing he could do.

40

Morgantown, WV

It began with dreams; intense, vivid dreams of the Buddha and Buddhist iconography, Bodhi trees, and lotus flowers.

At first Brook thought it was a side effect of meditation, something she had decided to try again even though she was sure she never did it right. She had hoped it would calm her and ease her pain, as well as an excuse to refuse Tom's constant urging to get back into therapy.

"They'll just put me on more meds," Brook scoffed the last time he'd mentioned it. "I'll be a zombie again."

"There are new drugs coming out all the time," Tom argued. "It's not a one-size fits all situation. Sometimes it takes some experimenting to find the right combination."

"What are you, a psychiatrist?" Brook asked.

"No, but I read things."

"I'm meditating, leave me alone. It's working, okay?" Brook had said, ending the conversation, at least for a while, though privately she knew it wasn't helping—not really.

Now, she wondered if she'd been wrong about that assessment. Meditation had become something different in her brain, a journey through a mystical sea of illusion. She could travel anywhere at any time, feeling the warm bath of existence beneath her as she held a giant parasol over her head to protect her from harm and journeyed along the great Dharma wheel.

In scientific terms, she understood her brain's chemistry was changing, but in her heart, she knew she was heading toward total enlightenment, eternal harmony; the complete purity of mind, body, and spirit—the shedding of the flesh, the abandonment of illusion and stress, and the exile of fear and desire.

Tom sensed a change in Brook, too, but wasn't convinced it was for the better. She seemed less grounded and more mercurial.

Brook had started trying to translate the linen-bound book handwritten in Tocharian that he had taken from the bookshop in Amman. She then graduated to spending hours on the Internet researching Eastern religious thought, along with its drawings and paintings. Still refusing to leave the house, she'd regularly send Tom to the local library for various sacred texts. She'd like to have tapped the university library system, but that was off-limits to her now.

At first, Tom had been encouraged, thinking that Brook's curiosity had hooked onto some lost treasure she meant to find for the benefit of the planet and to reinstate her position as one of the world's foremost archaeologists. This encouragement dwindled as her clothes changed, swiftly followed by her hairstyle and her attitude. She was no longer possessed by crying jags, panic attacks, or days of depression when she refused to get of bed; but now her stare was blank, as if there was nothing on this Earth worth seeing.

"Gone native," Tom mumbled to himself as he watched Brook float through rooms in her loose fitting sari. She now insisted on a diet of Asian food—either takeout or from mixes Tom got at the store—lots of curries, masalas, *daal*, chickpeas, and yogurt. Meat was banned from the house except for Saqqara's dog food.

Whatever it was, the change seemed to be working as far as Brook was concerned.

Tom wasn't so sure.

One morning, she made an announcement:

"I'm moving to Tibet," she told Tom.

"Tibet?" Tom managed, stunned.

"That's right," she stated pleasantly, enjoying Tom's reaction. "I'm going to Tibet to teach. I don't think I'm supposed to call it 'Tibet', but 'Autonomous Region of the People's Republic of China' is such a mouthful, don't you think?"

"I do."

"I'll be teaching English," Brook explained. "In Lhasa, population three hundred thousand—I looked it up. They think anybody who can speak English can teach it—even disgraced archaeologists."

"Huh..." was all Tom could say. In his mind, she was leaving him. He'd been ready for that, but still, it was a shock.

"But that's the beauty of it," Brook went on. "They have no idea; they've never even heard of me!"

She laughed.

Tom smiled, and held back tears. *She hasn't laughed like this since...Moscow.*

"When do you leave?" Tom asked, choking a little as he spoke.

"As soon as we can get our visas in order and get on a plane," Brook told him. "They want us right away."

"Us?" Tom managed, shocked.

"Of course, silly, you need to teach. You can't just be sitting around all day using up what little oxygen they have up there. Plus, I think it's time you and I got married, don't you?"

Tom said nothing, but looked on, dumbfounded. Now he *knew* Brook was crazy.

41

Lhasa, Tibet

It wasn't quite seven years in Tibet, but after six months Lhasa was starting to feel like home. Brook and Tom had quickly found jobs teaching English and Brook had even applied for a position leading an archeological expedition in the Himalayas.

The morning was Brook's favorite part of the day. Their house had an east-facing view and watching the sun rise over the mountains, had her feeling optimistic about her future again.

One morning, on the day it all changed, Brook sat in the living room sipping her coffee and reading the news from back home. Tom worked in the kitchen, preparing breakfast. Brook skimmed the headlines of the lead stories, ignoring anything political, until something caught her eye.

"Do you feel like one egg or two this morning?" came a call from the kitchen.

Brook grunted back an inaudible response.

"Brook?" Tom called out again. This time, there was no reply; Brook was so focused on the story in front of her that his voice didn't even register.

"Earth to Brook..." Tom repeated a little louder, elongating the pronunciation of her name as if he was calling a disobedient child.

Where he expected to hear a reply, Tom thought he heard the sound of breaking glass. Alarmed, he called out again and came out of the kitchen peering into the living room.

Brook's favorite coffee cup, a souvenir from a museum back home in America, had smashed on the ground, shattering into dozens of little pieces, and her morning coffee had spilled all over the floor. Brook sat still, transfixed by what she was reading, and completely oblivious to what had happened around her.

Concerned, Tom walked over and peered over her shoulder to see what she was looking at.

Mysterious tomb discovered in Egypt—Chinese-led archeological team set to make a "major announcement"

A team of archeologists in Egypt has confirmed they are set to make a major announcement after making a "stunning" discovery at a construction site near Alexandria.

The team's lead, Chinese archeologist Dr. Song Cheung, confirmed they have located a 2,000-year-old ancient tomb, containing a mysterious sarcophagus made entirely of granite.

"We believe it to be the biggest sarcophagus ever found," Dr. Song said.

In addition, the team found a number of alabaster sculptures, dating back to the Ptolemaic period (305-30 BC). The team will now work with the

Egyptian Ministry of Antiquities to recover all of the items and potentially open the tomb. Although the contents of the tomb remain a mystery for now, the promise of a major announcement has left some on social media speculating it might be the long-lost tomb of Alexander the Great.

Following the discovery of Cleopatra's tomb by American Brook Burlington, the whereabouts of Alexander remains one of Egypt's last great mysteries.

"I have to go, Tom. I have to be a part of this," Brook said slowly.

Tom smiled, wrestling mixed emotions—while he had a fleeting worry about Brook's ability to handle the pressure of being involved with another major dig, he couldn't help but be excited by seeing a glimpse of the woman he fell in love with back in Egypt. He knew how much archeology meant to her, to both of them.

"No, Brook," he replied, "we're a team now, and *we* have to be a part of this. You start packing, I'll clean up."

Brook snapped back to life, gave Tom a hug, and invigorated by the possibility of a new discovery, she practically skipped out of the room. She emerged a few minutes later with a beaming smile, bags fully packed and grabbed her mobile phone, dialing quickly. It was morning in Tibet, evening in the United States.

After what seemed like forever, the call connected, and Brook spoke with an excitement in her voice that Tom hadn't heard in months.

"Professor Green? It's Brook Burlington… fancy another trip to Egypt?"

FACT OR FICTION?

The Lost Library of the Tsar is a work of entertainment. Names, characters, places and incidents are products of the author's imagination. Any resemblance to actual events, locations and persons is coincidental. Having said all of that, Brook's adventures are deep-rooted in historical mysteries and it's important to call out where the line between fact and fiction lies.

Almost all of the major players in the novel—Brook, Tom, Professor Green, Lev, Pejna and Strelov (both generations) are fictional characters.

The Lost Library of Ivan the Terrible, also known as the Golden Library, is supposedly real, although it remains undiscovered. The contents of the library are thought to be rare Greek, Latin and Egyptian works. The library's location is rumored to be under the Kremlin and has been sought after for hundreds of years. Napoleon was among those who were supposedly fascinated by discovering the library. In the 1700s Russian Tsar Peter the Great attempted to locate the library, believing its contents would contain treasures that would help the country's treasury after being involved in war for several years.

Ivan himself is an infamous and fascinating character. He was an autocrat who killed his eldest son and heir, horribly mismanaged his country's economy, conquered territories and waged wars, but despite all that, he seems to have been an intelligent man, a talented poet, and a firm supporter of the arts. Under his watch, the printing press was introduced to Russia. It is entirely plausible, then, that he would have a secret library of his own, containing some of the world's greatest written works. One interesting tidbit, which I ultimately cut from the book, was that the use of the term "Terrible" had a very different context in Ivan's time. Rather than Terrible in the way we know it today, it more accurately translates to dangerous and powerful and keeping enemies in fear.

Stelletski, who Valeri Strelov meets, was a real person. A *New York Times* article printed in 1929 reported that Stelletski found archives showing "two large rooms filled with treasure chests known to exist under the Kremlin."

The Amelia Edwards Chair title Brook is awarded then stripped of is based on the Edwards Professor of Egyptian Archaeology and Philology, a position at University College London. At the time of writing, Professor Stephen Quirke, Curator of the Petrie Museum in London, holds the position. Edwards herself is a 19th-century writer and Egyptologist. Her most famous work was *A Thousand Miles Up the Nile,* which charted her journey to Abu Simbel in the southern part of the country.

T.E. Lawrence (better known as Lawrence of Arabia) is one of the most interesting historical figures of the last 100 years. During World War I he played a role as an advisor to Price Feisal in the revolt against Turkish rule. As mentioned in Chapter 3, Lawrence did present a rifle King George V a rifle after the war. However, the story about Isa and his special shotgun with the burn box is fiction.

The history of Kurdistan is complex and any explanation I offered would not do it justice. In the Treaty of Sevres, Kurdistan was scheduled to have a referendum to decide its fate. Of course, that never happened. I'm not sure of the why – it seems that there was never consensus on what the borders should be, and as such no proposals were ever taken forward. It seems likely that any Kurdish state would have contained areas within current-day Iraq and Turkey, hence Mehmet's involvement. Suffice it to say, any document that surfaced now confirming that area's right to independence could have major implications. I've intentionally tried to avoid the political side of that story.

Edward Noel was a real person. Maxwell's description of him being a 'British officer and spy' is accurate. During the Great War he was based in Persia (Iran) and it was not a stretch to imagine he might have been given the title of Ambassador to Kurdistan. The anecdote about Noel smuggling Russian General Peter Polovstov out of Russia is real.

I've never been to Amman, so I don't know if there is a book store there called al-Nasrani's. I assume there isn't. If there is, be sure to go in – the owner might have some interesting stories for you...

AUTHOR'S NOTES

As writers, we are often told to write what we know.

In many ways, Brook's path in this book mirrors my own in the year since *The Lost Tomb of Cleopatra* was completed. Her battles with imposter syndrome at the start of the book aligned with my own overwhelming sense of nervousness and vulnerability in the days after I pushed 'Publish' for the first time in March 2018. I have been very humbled by the response to the first book and the support I received – I tried to portray some of that humility and inner conflict in Brook's narrative throughout this part of her journey.

Thank you to the very talented Lauren Whale, who does an amazing job editing my work. I am excited to continue to have you as my professional partner-in-crime on all Brook's future adventures. A special thank you to my father—who remains my biggest fan and most honest critic—Jaclyn, for being my inspiration every single day, and the entire Whincup family.

Most of all, I want to thank you, the reader, for supporting this project and the works of other independent writers like me. I know how many options there are for your time and attention these days, and I appreciate everyone who has taken the time to read the book and advocate for it; especially those of you who choose to add a kind review to Amazon or Goodreads. Those words help other people find the book, and they mean more than you realize.

Stay tuned for *The Lost Tomb of Alexander the Great,* coming in early 2019.

ABOUT THE AUTHOR

JT Osbourne is an Amazon best-selling author who specializes in stories that combine historical fiction and modern-day adventure. His debut novel, *The Lost Tomb of Cleopatra,* has sold over 10,000 copies worldwide, and hit number one in two Amazon categories.. Always fascinated by the Grand Tour, JT has visited over 50 countries, cruised the Nile, climbed Mt. Kilimanjaro and Mt. Fuji, and has searched for lost tombs in Egypt. Wherever his travels take him, he'll always consider Toronto, Canada, where he lives with his husky, Simba, home.

Printed in Great Britain
by Amazon

32697811R00160